BETWEEN THE COVERS

A MET HIS MATCH SPIN-OFF NOVEL

LOUISA MASTERS

Between the Covers

Copyright © 2020 by Louisa Masters

Cover Designer: Booksmith Designs

All rights reserved.

No part of this book may be reproduced in any form or by any means without the prior written consent of the author, excepting brief quotes used in reviews.

Please do not participate in or encourage piracy of copyrighted materials in violation of the author's rights. Purchase only authorized editions.

This is a work of fiction. Names, characters, places, events and incidents either are the product of the author's imagination or are used fictitiously, and any resemblance to persons, living or dead, business establishments, events or locales is entirely coincidental.

To the extent that the image or images on the cover of this book depict a person or persons, such person or persons are merely models and are not intended to portray any character or characters featured in the book.

Paperback ISBN 978-0-6483374-7-8

ABOUT BETWEEN THE COVERS

Love is complicated. Do it anyway.

For two years, Dani Novak has lived vicariously through her best friend while slogging away at work and caring for her ill grandmother. But with her grandmother's passing, a world of opportunity opens to her—if only she has the courage to seize it.

Publicly, Malik al-Saud is a wealthy, spoiled jet setter, but behind the scenes, he works hard at his vocation. Secretly a best-selling author, Malik struggles to keep his work separate from his playboy reputation—and above all, stay out of his disapproving father's way.

They've been getting to know each other through his cousin and her best friend. Now, finally, it's time for them to meet. It doesn't take long for friendship to turn to more—but when Malik's family issues interfere, things get ugly. Can they manage these unexpected complications? Dani fears that Malik's lifelong antagonism with his family is insurmountable.

CHAPTER ONE

Dani wandered aimlessly through the house. From the kitchen into the living room, through the opening to the entryway, down the hall past the bedrooms, and back into the kitchen. And then she did it again, walking slowly, pausing every so often to touch or stare.

Her home had never felt so empty.

She'd lived in this house for three years and never had a roommate here, never felt lonely. She loved living alone. But after being surrounded by people for the last two days, being alone felt wrong.

Or maybe it was just that she'd never see her gran again.

Sinking into her granddad's old armchair—the one her gran had given her when she first moved out on her own, and that they had spent hours together choosing new fabric for—she sighed. They'd—*she'd*—known for a long time that this day was coming. Gran had been poorly for years, and the last six months she'd needed actual full-time nursing care. It was only due to the generosity of Dani's best friend that they'd been able to accede to Gran's wishes and not have her admitted to a nursing home. Instead they'd been able to hire round-the-clock nurses to look after her at home.

Dani sighed again. She wished Ben was here and not halfway around the world in Monaco. When a girl lost her gran, she really needed her BFF.

Maybe she should go back to Gran's place. Her mum was there still, with a steady stream of visitors dropping in to pay their respects. Dani had been there herself for over a week, ever since the nurse had told them to be prepared. The last two days, since… well, she'd wished herself anywhere else. Her mother had only sent her home an hour ago with a sharp order to get some rest.

She snorted. If only. Sitting down to rest meant giving herself time to think, to remember, to *feel*. She would a thousand times prefer to serve coffee to condolence-givers, talk with the priest, and sort through photos for a montage. Not to mention the dozens of other little details nobody even considered until they were necessary.

The doorbell rang, and she leaped to her feet with a rush of gratitude. She didn't even care who it was—most likely her brother, but she'd happily welcome a salesman, evangelist, or axe murderer. It took only seconds to unlock the door and yank it open, and—

She burst into tears.

"Oh, hey now," Ben said as he wrapped her in his arms. She clung to him, sobbing harder than she could ever remember. She'd been so proud of how she'd restrained her tears. She hadn't wanted to burden her parents or siblings with her grief, not when they all shared it. But now she had her bestie's shoulder to cry on.

"Take her inside. It's cold." The soft, French-accented words were her first indication that Ben had not arrived alone, and even as Ben ushered her back into the house—which was not much warmer, since she'd forgotten to turn on the heater when she got home—she sucked in a sob and raised her head.

Léo's gorgeous face smiled kindly at her. "I am so sorry for your loss, Dani," he said, following them through the door and closing it behind him. Sniffling, she swiped tears from her face.

"Thank you. And thank you so, so much for coming." She leaned back against Ben and let him support her. She'd known she missed him, that she wanted him here, but not how much. Not until she'd opened the door and seen him.

"Like we wouldn't have." Ben snorted. "Please. I would have come months ago to nurse Gran Carol myself if you hadn't told me no." He took her hand and led her into the living room. "Jesus, Dan, it's freaking freezing in here. Sit. I'm going to turn on the heater." He pushed her down into the armchair and hustled back into the corridor, where the thermostat and controls were. Léo looked around and took a seat on the small—very small—sofa. He was dressed casually—for him—but still looked just as out of place this time as he had when they last visited, just before Christmas.

"How have you been?" she asked inanely, and instantly wanted to kick herself. She knew exactly how he'd been. She and Ben spoke, texted, or FaceTimed nearly every day. The moment anything vaguely interesting happened in any of their lives, it got shared. She felt closer to Léo, his cousin, and their friends than she did to some of the people she saw and spoke to every day, even though she'd only met Léo in person twice and the others not at all.

But she just didn't know what to say.

"I'm well," Léo said gently. "Have you eaten? Rested?"

She shrugged, listening to the thumping sounds Ben was making as he went through her kitchen cupboards. Finally he came back out, glaring. "Call Malik," he told Léo. "We need the car back to go grocery shopping. Dani, when was the last time you cooked?"

Dani traced a finger over the arm of her chair. "I've been spending most of my time at Gran's the last few weeks," she admitted, trying to block out exactly *why*. Wait…. "Did you say Malik?" She glanced over at Léo, who was talking softly into his phone. "Léo's cousin Malik?"

"Yeah." Ben perched beside her on the chair arm, crowding her in the best possible way. "He went with our luggage to check in to the hotel." He stroked his hand over her hair, and she leaned into it.

The fog in Dani's head was pretty thick, had been for days, but there was still something about Malik being there that didn't compute.

"Why?"

"What do you mean, why? We didn't want to just leave the car and driver sitting outside your house, and Malik thought it might be better for you if it was just me and Léo tonight."

She shook her head. "No, I mean… why is Malik here at all? In Australia?"

Ben huffed, leaned over, and kissed the top of her head. "He came to offer his support, Dani. Because you're my best friend, and he's gotten to know you a bit and you've given us your support. Lucien and Si were coming too, but something came up with the charity like, literally two minutes before we boarded the plane. We left them at the airport."

Her sinuses burned as tears welled up again. "Wha—?" she managed to choke out, and Ben slid into the chair properly, pulling her into his lap and wrapping his arms around her.

"Oh, baby. You do nice things for people, and they want to be there for you when you need it." He held her close once more as she sobbed. She hadn't cried at all in the past two days, not until Ben arrived and told her that people she hardly knew wanted to give her support. It made something in her chest burn, but in a good way.

Léo and Ben spoke quietly over her head, but even after she was done crying, she didn't bother to listen, just lay limp against Ben's chest and let her thoughts float through the numb gray fog in her head.

Eventually she felt herself being lifted, and she raised her head to find herself in Léo's arms, being carried toward the door.

"What…?" Forming the entire question was too much work, but fortunately Léo understood.

"We are taking you to our hotel," he said. "You can have room service and be looked after and Ben will stay with you. He is packing you a bag now."

Some part of her wanted to protest at not being consulted, but oh, how lovely it would be to sleep in a big bed with her bestie and eat food she wouldn't have to prepare and just forget this day and the ones before and those yet to come.

She laid her head against Léo's shoulder and closed her eyes. "Okay." They were outside now, but sometime when she hadn't been paying attention, someone—Ben?—had draped a blanket over her, so the cold barely touched her. A moment later, she was being laid in the back seat of a car. She snuggled into the corner, pulling the blanket tighter around herself.

"Is she okay?" a voice asked quietly, and Dani wanted to open her eyes and see the face she knew went with that voice, but her lids were too heavy.

"Hi, Malik," she muttered, the words a little slurred.

"Hello, Dani." A warm hand stroked hair away from her face. "Rest. We'll take care of you."

Sleep enveloped her.

❧

HER FIRST AWARENESS was of being warm. She was surrounded by soft, fluffy warmth, rested and comfortable.

Then it all came rushing back, and she opened her eyes. An unfamiliar ceiling came into focus, followed a moment later by Ben's face.

"You're awake. Want some breakfast?"

Dani nodded. If she spoke, she might cry again. She just needed a few moments to get herself together. The bed shifted and Ben disappeared, and a second later she heard a door close. Breathing deeply, she sat up and stared fixedly at the white sheets until the tears receded, then lifted her head and looked around.

Fuck me.

She'd never get used to the fact that Ben, her BFF who hated to spend a cent he didn't need to and who until pretty recently considered twenty dollars for a pair of jeans "kind of expensive," now was not only rich in his own right but had hooked up with a guy who redefined the term super-freak-ing-wealthy. Case in point, this hotel room that was almost the same size as her two-bedroom house, and definitely better decorated. Was it even allowed for a hotel to have real artwork instead of mass-produced prints?

Sighing, she got up, picked up her robe, which Ben had thoughtfully draped over the end of the bed, and wrapped herself in it. She must have been really out of it last night, because she'd been changed out of her clothes and into her flannel pj's without ever waking. Not surprising, really, since she'd not been sleeping well. It was hard to switch her mind off and forget that Gran….

Well. It would get easier, she knew that, and until then, she just had to keep on.

She crossed the room and properly opened the drapes,

which had just been cracked enough to provide dim light. Winter sunshine flooded in, momentarily blinding her. When her vision cleared, she gasped. The view! Whichever hotel they were in, they were on a seriously upper floor, and the view over the city and to the bay beyond was fabulous. She'd stayed in a few city hotel rooms in her time, and she only ever got a view of busy streets or the buildings opposite. If this was what money could buy, maybe she should get used to Ben having it.

The sound of a door opening had her turning to see Ben poke his head in. "You're up! Breakfast should be here in about twenty minutes. Terry made coffee if you want some."

"Sure, I just need— Wait. Who's Terry?"

Ben pulled a face, came into the room, and closed the door. "The butler. It's kind of weird having him here, but Léo and Malik are totally fine with it, like it's normal."

Dani tipped her head to the side, trying to make sense of that. "There's a butler?" Had she misunderstood? Were they in a private home, not a hotel? But *whose*?

"Yeah, the suite comes with twenty-four-hour butler service. I probably wouldn't ever have thought of using it, because... butler? But Léo called him before I was even up this morning. He makes really great coffee."

Right. Of course. They were in a hotel suite that had twenty-four-hour butler service. She shook her head to clear it. "I just need to use the bathroom," she told Ben, and he pointed to another door.

When she emerged from the bedroom, having used the facilities, showered, and dressed in the ratty old track pants and jumper Ben had packed for her, she was surprised to find herself in a corridor, not the main room of the suite. How freaking big was this thing? She peeked into doors as she passed them and found a small office and a dining room before she reached the living area. She could see another corridor at the other end.

"Dani." Léo stood from the couch and crossed over to her, bending to kiss her cheek. He studied her face. "You look better rested."

"I slept right through," she told him. "Thank you for this."

He smiled and took her arm, leading her over to sit in a comfortable armchair. "Anything we can do, Dani, is yours. Would you like some coffee?"

"Yes, please." It was all she could say. How did you respond when the superwealthy and influential son of a princess told you he'd do anything for you? If he weren't gay and in love with her bestie, it would be a Harlequin romance novel come to life.

Léo looked around, and as if by magic, a tall, slim man appeared from the other corridor and asked for her coffee order. Presumably this was Terry, but Dani was too surprised by his seeming psychic ability to ask, and by the time her brain kicked into gear, he'd delivered her latte and disappeared again.

That was some trick.

"Ben has gone to fetch Malik," Léo volunteered, watching as she sipped. "Breakfast will be here shortly."

He'd barely finished speaking when there was the sound of a door opening somewhere in the suite, and a moment later Ben came in, followed by Malik.

"—being ridiculous. You always order that for breakfast," Ben declared impatiently.

"At home, yes. But perhaps here I wanted something different. Or perhaps they will not make it the way I like it," Malik argued, and Dani took a moment to study him. They'd spoken many times, since Ben often included his friends in calls to her, and she'd done extensive internet research on him and Léo's friend Lucien when Ben had first started seeing Léo, but they'd never met in person.

He was just as ridiculously handsome as his cousin and was *also* a superwealthy and influential son of a princess. There should be a law against that—it just wasn't fair to her poor, neglected girly parts.

Ben huffed and rolled his eyes, then spotted her and promptly abandoned the discussion. "Good coffee?" he asked, smirking.

"The best," she replied drily. "Terry's a genius. Good morning, Malik."

"Hello, Dani." He came over and bent to kiss her cheek, then studied her in much the same way Léo had. It was uncanny. "Did you sleep well?"

"I did, thank you. And thank you so much for coming all this way. It…." *Fuck.* She blinked back the tears burning her sinuses. "It means a lot."

"Family matters," he said quietly, and then the heavy moment was blessedly interrupted by a doorbell.

"That will be breakfast," Léo said, but nobody moved. Dani blinked. Should she…?

She heard the door opening. Ah. Of course, Terry would have gone. This having a butler thing might be cool, after all.

CHAPTER TWO

Malik stood at the priest's behest and listened to the words of the Catholic mass. It was far from the first time he'd attended a Catholic funeral—his uncle's position in European society came with many friendships and obligations, and having been practically raised in the Artois home, Malik had been included in many of them.

This funeral was not held in a cathedral and overseen by a bishop. The parish church held only a few hundred people, and the priest had obviously known Carol personally. But the mass itself, the hymns, and the overwhelming aura of heaviness that grief brought—those things remained the same.

Several rows ahead, Dani stood with her parents and siblings, Ben a stalwart comfort at her side. It had been Dani's mother who had insisted Ben sit with them, claiming that Carol had loved him as though he were one of her grandchildren, and the rest of the family had been quick to agree. Dani had clung to her best friend, and Ben had been helpless to refuse—not that Malik thought he had wanted to. He had been grieving too, ever since he'd gotten the news, and although Malik had initially thought this trip would be about providing support for Dani, it hadn't taken him long to realize Ben desperately needed the comfort of his best friend also.

As the priest came down from the altar to give communion, Léo rose. In his younger years, Malik had often joined the line and received a blessing, but that had stopped when his father had found out and had a conniption fit. Malik had only ever participated to keep from sitting alone in the pew, and it hadn't been worth the drama he would have to deal with to continue doing so. Personally, he didn't see why it mattered. Neither he nor Léo was religious in any way—it was just a part of the mass they attended out of social obligation.

The communion hymn came to an end, and there was the quiet rustle of people shifting as the priest approached the microphone.

"And now Carol's grandchildren would like to say a few words," he said softly, and Dani, her brother, and her sister all rose and moved toward the altar.

Malik had always found the concept of eulogies to be horrible. They were either terribly sad, exposing the grief of the speaker even when happy anecdotes were shared, or they were clinical in a way that stripped humanity from the deceased and portrayed them as mere facts. This eulogy was no different—the love Carol's grandchildren had felt for her was evident in every word, every story told, and by the time it was Dani's turn to speak, her brother and sister had both broken down.

"My gran was a woman who knew what she wanted. And if she didn't know in any particular moment, she knew that it was important to find out. The advice she gave me most frequently was to determine what it was I wanted from everything in life, even if I didn't think I cared. 'Life, Dani, is too short to not care about things.' As you've already heard, she was bluntly honest, sometimes to the point of what others considered rudeness, and that was purely because she didn't see the point in wasting time or effort on social subterfuge—but if it brought her happiness, she would spend hours on the most trivial of things. And the thing that made her happy above all others was happiness in those she loved.

"When I was a little girl, I was obsessed with braiding friendship bracelets, so much so that it drove my family to distraction. Gran would spend hours doing it with me. It wasn't until I reached adulthood that I discovered that she loathed braiding of any kind." Dani paused, biting her lip, and Malik realized she was struggling to maintain her composure. "She spent huge chunks of time doing something she absolutely hated because"—her voice caught—"because it made me happy." She paused again and took a deep breath.

"I asked her about it once, why she hadn't tried to steer me toward another activity, or even just left me to do it alone —after all, it wasn't an activity that required two people. She just smiled at me and said—" The pause this time was longer, and a tear ran down each cheek, but when her brother stepped forward, Dani held up a hand and continued, her voice choked. "She said that if she'd done that, she never would have gotten to see me be so happy, and being witness to my joy was worth anything." She exhaled, and when she spoke again, her voice was steady. "That's the thing I will always remember about Gran. She worked to get what she wanted, no matter what it cost her, and what she wanted more than anything was for her family to be happy. Gran, I know you know that you succeeded. Today we grieve, but when we remember you, it will be with happy thoughts. You got what you wanted, and we love you all the more for it."

As the congregation sniffled, the three siblings stepped down from the altar. Dani's face, half hidden by the sweep of her dark hair, was set, but once she resumed her seat, she dropped her head, covering her face with her hands, and her shoulders shook.

A short time later, the recessional began, and Malik automatically bowed his head in respect as the casket was carried past. He lifted his gaze in time to catch sight of Dani's tearstained, puffy face as she followed it, an arm around her mother. For just a second, their gazes met, and in Dani's brown eyes he saw the qualities he imagined her grandmother must have had—strength, determination, and compassion so vast it could not be measured. Today she grieved, but she would not let grief take her over.

And damned if that didn't stir something in him that was best left alone.

&a.

"FUNERALS SUCK," Dani declared, dropping onto her parents' couch next to Ben and leaning against him. She sighed and closed her eyes, kicking off the ridiculously uncomfortable black heels she'd been wearing all day. Considering how staid and ugly they were, they shouldn't hurt her feet anywhere near as much as they did.

Ben dropped a kiss on the top of her head. "I know. It's done now."

And it was. There had been a lovely turnout for her gran at the church, the cemetery, and the quiet wake held in the function room of a local restaurant after, but now all the mourners were gone and it was just family—her parents, siblings, Ben, Léo, and Malik.

Even this was exhausting. She wanted to go home—well, back to the hotel. She didn't actually want to go home, and that was freaking her out. Her home was her sanctuary but being there meant being alone. That had never bothered her before, and she wasn't sure she really wanted to think about why it did now. But she would have to go home eventually. And on that note….

"When do you leave?" Opening her eyes, she sat upright and looked at Ben expectantly.

He pouted. "Sick of me already?"

She shoved his arm. "Yes. I can't wait to get rid of you. Seriously, how long can you stay?"

"As long as you want us here." He shrugged. "Léo can work from anywhere, and I called the agency before I left and told them not to line anything up until further notice." Despite having inherited a pile of cash from a former client, Ben still liked to work as a nurse on an as-needed basis. His busy little brain needed something to stave off the boredom of being rich and idle.

"And Malik?" she asked, watching from across the room as he spoke quietly with Léo and her dad. They all looked quite serious, but then Malik said something, that charming smile flashing, and they laughed softly.

Ben shrugged again. "If he needs to go back, he will. But I don't think he's on a schedule."

Still studying those cut-glass cheekbones and nicely shaped mouth, she asked, "Does he do anything?"

A dirty-sounding *he-he-he* was Ben's response, and she elbowed him in the side. "You know what I mean."

"Ow. Yeah, I know. I have no idea. I mean, he and Léo do a lot of stuff together, but sometimes he's busy with other things. I never asked if he has a job, and nobody ever said."

Dani wrinkled her nose. "That's not very nice, Benji. You should know those sorts of things about the people you're close to."

Ben groaned, but when she glanced over at him, he was smiling. "I never thought I'd be glad to hear you call me Benji," he said, and she shrugged. She hadn't felt much like teasing him the last few days, but the funeral, as difficult as it had been, had given her some closure.

"Listen"—Ben straightened and turned more fully toward her—"I want you to think about something."

"I'm always thinking," she quipped automatically, then blinked. It felt kind of weird to joke, but also weird that it wasn't more weird. Her gran was gone, and it had left a gaping hole in her chest—shouldn't it feel wrong to crack jokes?

Ben flicked the side of her face with his forefinger. "Stop *over*thinking," he admonished. "I can almost hear the wheels in your brain turning. Let me say this right now: it is not a bad thing for you to feel happy. It doesn't take away from your love for Gran Carol and your grief over losing her if you're not miserable for every second of every day. And she would be furious with you if she thought you didn't want to be happy just because she's gone. Got it?" The stern expression on his face made her heart melt. Ben was such a dork most of the time that she sometimes forgot how very good he was at looking after people.

She snuggled up to him and rested her head on his shoulder. "Got it. It does feel a little weird not to be sad every second, but I knew that kind of constant grief wouldn't last forever. I just have to get used to it all, I guess."

Ben ruffled her hair. "Good. And while you're sorting through your emotions and taking ownership of them"—she snorted—"I want you to think about coming back to Monaco with us."

Dani shot upright so fast that her skull cracked against Ben's chin. Their resulting howls brought her mum, brother, and sister racing out of the kitchen and had Léo crossing the room in two long strides.

"What is *wrong* with you?" Ben moaned, working his jaw as Léo leaned over to inspect it.

"Me?" she gasped, rubbing her head. "I'm not the one dropping bombshells!"

"What bombshell?" her brother asked curiously.

"Do either of you need ice?" her mum offered.

Dani and Ben assured everyone that they were fine, and the group mostly dispersed, with Léo and Malik joining them—Léo on the couch next to Ben, and Malik in the armchair kitty-corner to Dani.

"I can't believe you were that surprised," Ben grumbled, leaning against Léo.

Dani huffed. "How could I *not* be surprised? One minute we're talking about grief, and the next you're saying you want me to pick up and jet around the world!"

"Ben said 'jet around the world'?" Malik asked skeptically, but Dani was too busy glaring at her bestie to reply.

Ben glared right back at her. "I did not say 'jet around the world,' nor did I mean that. I just suggested that you think about coming home with us, where you can spend time decompressing and working through your grief away from all the sources of stress in your life. How is that a bad thing?"

"This is fun," Malik said, presumably to Léo. Dani was locked in a stare down and couldn't check. "Do you think they'll start calling each other names next?"

"I can't just drop everything in my life and swan off to Monaco," she declared.

"Why not?" Ben challenged.

"We need popcorn," Malik said.

"Shut up, Malik." Léo's voice trembled with barely restrained... laughter?

"Because! My family needs me. I have a job that I can't just take time off from. I have a mortgage and... and... I have friends who would miss me!" The words were no sooner out of her mouth than she regretted them. Ben's face changed, hurt written all over his expression. Even Malik was silent.

"You have friends who'd miss you more than I have these past couple years?" The words were a challenge, but his tone was pure misery. Dani sighed.

"No. Nobody would miss me as much as you have, or as much as I've missed you." It was the truth. Ben was such an essential, interwoven part of her life that she could not conceive of him not being in it. While she would never want to deny him the happiness and love he'd found with Léo, the years since he'd moved to Monaco had been so hard—even though they were in touch every day.

Ben sighed. "Look. I know why you didn't come on the odyssey with me. You didn't want to leave Gran Carol. I get it, and I would never have pressured you to do otherwise. I *didn't* pressure you, not anytime in these past two years, not even when Gran Carol ca—" He snapped his mouth shut and looked guilty.

Dani made a face. "She called you and asked you to invite me, didn't she?" It wasn't really a surprise. Her gran had often said that Dani deserved a break, that she should go on holiday to visit Ben—she'd once even offered to pay the airfare if Dani couldn't afford it.

"Yeah," Ben admitted sheepishly. "And I thought about it. Not thought about inviting you, because I'd already done that, and anyway, since when would you ever need an invitation to come and see me, right? But she asked me to fake an emergency of some kind so you'd come—say that Léo and I were fighting, or something like that. Because that's how much she loved you and wanted you to have a holiday. And because I love you too, I actually thought about it, but in the end, I stupidly decided to respect your wishes."

"This is like that soap opera Lucien's ex used to be in," Malik marveled, and this time Dani couldn't hold in her snort of laughter.

"Lucien has an ex who was in a soap opera?" Ben asked, distracted, and Malik nodded.

"She wasn't in it for long, though. After the third time in a month that the plot contradicted itself, she quit."

"That's so… weird." Ben and Dani exchanged glances and burst into laughter, and for a moment, Dani completely forgot that she was sad. Then the grief closed in again, and she had to remind herself that it was okay to laugh—and that Gran would have *loved* knowing that someone she (kind of) knew had dated a soap opera actress who quit because the soap opera was too soap opera-ish.

She sighed as she flopped back against the couch and turned her head to study her bestie. "Thank you for not faking an emergency so I would come to visit. And thank you for caring so much that you actually considered it."

Ben smiled, but his eyes were sad. "I would do anything for you. I really, really want to get you away from here and give you some time to relax. Please?"

What was she doing? Why the hell shouldn't she go stay with Ben in Monaco for a few weeks? She had tons of leave time accrued at work. "Not right now." She held up a hand when Ben began to protest. "Later this year, okay? I can't just take off from work without warning, and the more notice I give them, the more time I can take off. So in September, maybe October, I'll come and spend a month. How's that sound?"

Ben hug-tackled her.

"Aww," Malik said. "Is this a group hug?"

Friends, new and old, were worth their weight in gold.

CHAPTER THREE

*M*alik got up to fetch another bottle of wine from the beautifully stocked wine fridge in the kitchen. He'd been quite surprised to find such a good selection—but then, he and Léo had stayed in this hotel before, years ago, and the best hotels tried to cater to their VIP guests' tastes.

He grabbed the bottle, hesitated, and then picked up a second one also. They'd already finished two, but Dani and Ben showed no signs of slowing down. This was actually the part of death that he coped best with—the drowning of emotion while the brain struggled to process. He'd helped many a friend wade through the initial post-funeral haze, whether it be with the assistance of alcohol or just the comfort of companionship. In this case, it was both. Dani had been stalwart for most of the past few days, crying only when they'd arrived and those few tears at the funeral, but since they'd opened the first bottle of wine, she'd allowed herself to break down more than once.

Sometimes, the security of a small group of friends and

the lowering of inhibitions did more to ease grief and provide closure than any ceremony could.

Rejoining the group, he picked up the corkscrew and efficiently opened one of the bottles.

"It always makes me so jealous when you and Léo do that," Ben declared, watching him from where he lay sprawled on the plush carpet, Dani's head resting on his stomach. "Every time I try to use a corkscrew, it either doesn't screw or I end up with bits of cork in the wine."

Malik tried not to laugh.

"Malik and I have been watching the very best sommeliers open wine since we were young," Léo offered, as though that made any difference. It seemed to placate Ben, though, who held out his wineglass demandingly, nudging Dani to sit up.

She propped herself against the coffee table and watched blankly while he filled her glass again. "Thank you," she said in an exhausted voice.

"De rien," he murmured—and her head snapped up so sharply that he nearly dropped the wine in surprise.

"Talk French to me!" she demanded, her voice much stronger. Malik shot Léo a questioning look, but just got a shrug in return.

"Pourquoi est-ce que je parle français?" he asked, and she grinned.

"Oh, that's easy! Um… *parce que j'ai besoin de pratiquer?*"

Her accent was terrible, and the way she made it seem like a question showed how unsure of her ability she was, but she had the words right and he couldn't help but smile.

"You've learned French!" Ben accused, and she laughed, but cut herself off sharply when the sound rang out. An odd kind of shock played over her face, and Malik rushed to distract her.

"Your grammar is very good," he said—in French. "How

long have you been learning?" He made sure to speak clearly and more slowly than usual.

She blinked a few times, no doubt still hung up on the shock and guilt of having laughed on the day of her grandmother's funeral. Grief was a funny thing—although he was certain that Dani's grandmother would have wanted her family to feel happiness again, grief had a way of warping that knowledge and digging its claws deep.

For a moment, he worried they would lose her to melancholy, but then she took a deep breath and replied, "A year and a half—since I knew Ben wasn't coming back to live." She spoke slowly, but Malik was sure that was just from lack of confidence. "I thought it would be best for when I visit."

"We appreciate it," Léo said. "We will speak only French when we are alone, so you can practice."

"Thank you," she replied promptly. "Please correct me when I make mistakes." She tilted her head. "I think I am pronouncing some things wrong." She pouted, clearly not happy with the idea.

Ben leaned over and gave her a smacking kiss on the cheek. "I hate that you never told me you were learning French," he told her, and then switched to English. "But the fact you did this reminds me so much of Gran Carol. It's just the kind of thing she'd do—spend over a year learning a new language so she could visit a friend in another country." He picked up his glass and raised it in salute. Dani's lip wobbled for a moment, but then she raised her glass also—and knocked back the contents.

"She loved the idea when I told her," she said quietly. "She was the one who helped me choose the app, and in the early days we did it together." She stared into space for long seconds, then shook her head and switched to French. "She was so excited to hear everything you were doing. She wanted to know everything about Léo, too—and you." She looked at Malik.

"Me?" he asked, surprised, and she nodded.

"Oh, yes. She loved gossip, and you did—caused gossip a lot."

Well, he couldn't argue with that. "I'm reformed," he said loftily, mostly because he knew it would make her smile, and at that second, he wanted to see that.

Sure enough, her face lit up, even as Ben snorted, and then Léo asked if her grandmother had ever been to France. She turned to answer him, and it felt to Malik as though the light in the room dimmed.

Oh, hell.

No. No way. He was not forming an infatuation for his cousin's boyfriend's best friend. A woman who was grieving. A woman who had always been funny, kind, and sweet, and who did not need or deserve his brand of chaos in her life.

And yet, as he watched the flash of her smile again, the sinking feeling in his stomach told Malik it was already too late.

GOING BACK to work felt both odd and wonderful. Gran had passed on a Saturday, and Dani had taken a full week off work to deal with the funeral arrangements and sorting out Gran's house. Her mother had told her it wasn't necessary, but Dani had seen the relief when she insisted. Some things just shouldn't have to be done alone.

But now, on this cold and miserable Monday morning—it wasn't even officially winter yet, but the weather was being nasty—Dani had left the luscious hotel suite to return to work. She had yet to go home, although she refused to admit there was a significant reason for that. She was just enjoying the time spent with her bestie, soaking up every second. Ben had pouted when she'd dressed for work and had tried to extract a promise that she'd meet him for lunch. Dani had hemmed and hawed, not knowing exactly what she'd find at the office. Theoretically, everything was set up to run smoothly in her absence, and she had an assistant-slash-intern to keep an eye on things, but… the truth was, Lisa, the intern, was a bit… flaky. In fact, she could almost be called inept. If it weren't for the fact that her father was a friend of the owner and had begged for a six-month work placement for her, there was no way in hell Dani would have kept her on. She was a nice enough girl, though a little shallow, but her incompetence was such that Dani had to review everything she did.

Which was why a niggle of apprehension was curling in her belly as she walked in through the main doors and waved at the receptionist, who was on a call. The cringe she got in response was her first indicator that something had happened.

Sighing, Dani made her way through the still mostly empty floor to her office. She'd been working for this printer and stationery supply company pretty much since she'd finished uni nearly eight years ago. The owner, an older gentleman called Harry, had hired her as a temporary receptionist. For Dani, it had been a stopgap job to make money while she hunted for something she really wanted. She was newly armed with a business degree, but not really sure how she wanted to apply it. That didn't mean she'd been about to half-ass the job, though, and within two weeks she'd overhauled several processes that made reception run much more efficiently. It hadn't taken her long to get bored, and she'd started poking around the rest of the office, picking up odd tasks the salesmen and admins didn't have time for. Before her three-month contract had run out, she'd had a better understanding of how the company worked than some of the senior execs, and Harry had basically told her to pick the job she wanted and he'd make sure she got trained for it if necessary. By then, she'd known exactly what that would be. Harry had created the office manager role, and together, in consultation with other staff, they'd redistributed duties in a way that kept Dani challenged and created deep gratitude amongst her colleagues. And she'd been happy for years.

It was only this year, since Harry had retired and his dick nephew had taken over, that tiny niggles of discontent had begun to settle in. The office dynamic had changed. A lot of longtime employees were not happy with the way "Dickhead Tom" was running things, and staff turnover had jumped in just a few months. Worse, the new people Tom was hiring didn't fit the core values Harry had spent so long instilling in the company. She and Tom had butted heads many times already about unnecessary and inefficient changes he wanted to make. At first, she'd respected his desire to put his own stamp on the company and had made suggestions that would make his changes practical, but he'd made it clear that her input was not wanted. He'd been running the place less than six months, and in the first quarter under his management, profit had already been down. The second quarter was only half done, but Dani knew it was going to be bad. If it wasn't for her dogged loyalty to the company and the remaining longtime staff, she'd already have been looking for another job—but how could she abandon them without trying her best to fix things?

She flipped on the light in her office and dumped her bag on her chair. Everything looked... fine. Neat. Tidy. In fact... untouched. Was that file in Lisa's in-tray the same one she'd left there over a week ago? Had Lisa not actioned it? She squinted around the room. Had Lisa even been in there while she was away?

A single knock on the open door preceded Kate, the receptionist. "Hey. How are you?" she asked with that you've-just-lost-a-loved-one sympathy Dani both appreciated and had been dreading. She smiled faintly.

"I'm okay. It's hard, but it wasn't unexpected."

Kate tipped her head. "If there's anything I can do...."

"Thank you. And thank you so much for sending flowers. They were lovely, and so thoughtful."

Kate nodded, sighed, and closed the door. Dani's stomach sank.

"There's something you should know before Lisa gets here."

Groan.

"Was she sick last week or something?" she asked. Could that be the reason her office looked like it had been locked and guarded for a week?

"Or something." Kate grimaced. "Keep your shit, yeah? Sometime since they both started working here, Tom and Lisa hooked up."

"What?"

"Shhh!" Kate looked nervously over her shoulder at the glass wall.

"Sorry." Dani lowered her voice, trying to process. "I'm just... surprised. He's, what, forty years older than her?"

"Closer to fifty." The twist to Kate's mouth made her feelings very clear. "We're trying not to judge, right?"

"That's right," Dani said firmly. "The age gap between them is none of our business." Having the CEO date an intern, though.... She made a mental note to check in with their HR team this morning. They must be going gonzo. Also, Tom was gross and a real dick. Lisa was cute, mostly sweet, and fun. It couldn't be money, could it? Her family was way richer than Tom, and— Oh, crap. "Does Harry know yet? And Lisa's family?" *This is not my problem,* she assured herself, even as she remembered Harry asking her to look out for Lisa. He'd meant it in a professional sense, right?

Kate shrugged. "I have no idea. Harry hasn't been in or anything. They basically just walked in on Wednesday holding hands, and then he pretty much ate her face off before he went into his office and she went to lunch."

Resisting the urge to gag at the image Kate had put into her head, Dani asked, "Wait—she arrived at the office and then went right out to lunch?" The faintly pitying look on Kate's face said it all. "Right. Well, that explains why nothing's been touched in here. Thanks for letting me know, Kate." Now what the hell was she supposed to do?

Kate left, and Dani booted up her computer, mindful of the glass wall and all her colleagues trickling in. She kept a calm smile on her face as several people wandered in to offer their condolences and tell her she'd been missed. One or two asked after Lisa, obviously fishing for gossip or hoping to drop a bomb on her, but Dani was the office manager for a reason. Those people were so efficiently managed back to their desks, they weren't even sure what had happened.

Still smiling, Dani began going through her emails, one eye on the time at the bottom of her screen. Lisa was late, which was not unusual, but today it presented Dani with more than the usual problem. How was she supposed to handle this? Pretend nothing was happening? Honestly, if this was someone else's workplace, she'd be agog for the gossip and not really give a fuck otherwise. Lisa wasn't her daughter or sister or her anything, after all, and if she wanted to be with a man who was old enough to be her grandfather and was a giant fucking prick, that was her business. Ditto for Tom. Although in other circumstances Dani couldn't really give a flying fuck who Tom hooked up with, except in a "I never want to think about Tom hooking up" way. But this…. Lisa was her intern. She was a senior manager in the company—all administrative staff reported to her, no matter which department they were assigned to—so she couldn't pass the buck. Tom was the CEO, and he was diddling a junior—very junior—member of her staff. She had to do *something*… she just wasn't sure what yet.

First, maybe review the HR policy manual? Call her friend from uni who specialized in employment law? Think of something to say to Lisa, because oh God, they just walked in and *fuck my life, that's disgusting!* Kate hadn't been wrong when she'd spoken about face-eating.

Choking back the bile that had risen to her throat, Dani shot a quick glance around the faces in the open-plan area of the office. Some were carefully blank, gazes averted. Some were disgusted. Some mixed shock with horror. Nobody looked happy, amused, or titillated, though. It wasn't the kind of kiss anyone ever wanted to see in a public space.

As the—barf—happy couple broke apart, Dani returned her attention to her emails. She'd checked in on her private address several times in the past week, despite being on leave, so it wasn't as out of control as it could have been. But the shared administrative inbox truly concerned her—it looked as though Lisa hadn't checked it at all, or if she had, she'd left a lot of emails unaddressed.

That was what needed to be handled first, Dani decided, just as Lisa strolled in.

"Good morning, Lisa," she said, hoping her tone was no different to what it would be on any other day. "I hope you had a good weekend. I have some questions for you about the admin inbox." There, that was professional, right? To the point, but still courteous.

"Hi, Dani." Lisa smiled brightly, and Dani was reminded again that she really was a sweet girl most of the time. She was just completely self-centered and not that bright. And clearly needed close supervision. "Tom wants to talk to you."

That threw her. *Say what?* Tom *wanted* to talk to her? Normally she had to practically tackle him in the hallway to get a minute with him.

"Uh, okay. Thanks for letting me know. Did he want me to set up a time, or—"

"Oh, no," Lisa assured her earnestly. "He said now."

Right. "Did he say why?" That wasn't professional at all, but neither was sending her intern to tell her he wanted a meeting rather than setting it up himself.

Lisa shook her head, and Dani stood. "I'll head over and see for myself, then. While I'm gone, can you get started on the admin inbox? And that file on your desk needs to be taken care of." She didn't say a word about how all of that *should* have been done last week, but her pointed look must have spoken volumes, because Lisa flushed.

On her way to Tom's office, she was waylaid twice, and only her determined stride and closed expression put off the others who tried to catch her attention. She still wasn't sure exactly how to address the whole "dating" Lisa thing with Tom, but if an opening came up, she'd take it and worry about the details in the moment.

Tom's PA, Julie, smiled widely at her as she approached, but Dani didn't need to be psychic to see the underlying note of desperation. Julie had been hired specifically when Tom came on board, Harry's assistant having retired when he did, and Dani had found her to be competent, capable, and utterly unimpressed with Tom as both a man and a manager. It wouldn't surprise anyone if she resigned.

"Good morning, Julie. Apparently, Tom wants to see me." Dani's tone conveyed her opinion of that. Julie nodded.

"He said as much as he went in," she replied, her tone conveying her opinion also. She stood, took the few steps to Tom's door, knocked perfunctorily, and then stuck her head in. "Dani's here." She stepped back and gestured for Dani to enter.

Since Tom had a glass wall looking out into the main office as well, announcing visitors was redundant. In Harry's day, Dani would have said hello to his assistant and then just knocked and announced herself. Tom liked a more formal, old-fashioned way of things—*right down to boinking the office intern, apparently.*

Dani smiled at Julie, walked in, and shut the door behind herself. Tom pretended to be absorbed in his computer screen, holding up a finger for her to wait—a tactic designed to establish him as the more important party and put her in her place. She had too much experience with big egos to be intimidated, so rather than hovering by the door awaiting his pleasure, she walked over to the visitor chair, made herself comfortable, and pulled out her phone. A quick check of the admin email inbox showed that Lisa was actually doing her job, so she switched to her message app and sent Ben a text.

My wanker boss is playing power games.

Men who need to play power games are lacking in power.

Well, you would know, being surrounded by powerful men.

Wow, can't believe I actually said that.

Me neither. I was just about to ask who had stolen your phone.

But you're not wrong ;-)

Whatcha doing?

Nothing interesting until you texted. Why's the wanker playing games?

Because he has a tiny dick and needs some way to feel important? How should I know?

How should you know his dick size? Don't want to think about the answer to that.

EW! That's disgusting. And also, why would a pretty, sweet, popular almost-teenager want to fuck a nearly 70yo gross dickhead?

OMG! WHAT IS HAPPENING THERE?

"Danika?" Tom's annoyed voice broke into the message she was composing. Casting a wistful glance at the screen, she hit Send halfway through her explanation and tucked the phone away. Ben would know it meant she'd been interrupted, and although he might be frustrated by the half message, he would wait for her to text again.

"Good morning, Tom," she said deliberately. "How was your weekend?"

He waved a hand, as though social pleasantries weren't worth his time. *Dick.* "I need to discuss something important with you."

Oh God, was he going to raise the subject of Lisa himself? Did she really want to hear it? Forcing a look of mild concern onto her face, she said, "Oh?"

Tom steepled his fingers. "I've been concerned about your work performance."

Everything in Dani froze. For a second, it was as though the universe had come to a standstill. And then it jolted back into action in a hot rush of fury. In her lap, her hands clenched into tight fists before she forced them to relax, and over the sound of her pounding heartbeat, she said, "What do you mean?" There was nothing about her work performance that warranted concern. Even with the massive personnel changes lately, the office still ran like clockwork. If this was another ploy of his to throw her off-balance, she was going to eviscerate him.

Slowly.

With a blunt object.

"It just seems that you're unable to cope with the changes I've been making in the company. You're set in your ways and unable to adapt." His smug tone made her itch all over, but she fought down her knee-jerk anger and defensiveness and forced herself to consider her response.

What is he doing?

There was no reason that she could see for him to be saying this. He couldn't sack her without three written warnings—which she didn't have, since her work and professionalism had always been up to standard—or unless she breached her terms of employment, which she knew she hadn't. He couldn't give her a poor performance evaluation, because all her job metrics showed that her performance was well above acceptable. So what was going on?

"I'm sorry you feel that way. I can assure you that I'm not opposed to change, and I believe I've been working with the staff to implement your changes as smoothly as possible." *You incompetent, dickless wanker.*

He shook his head, that smug expression still in place. "I disagree. In fact—"

"Disagree with what?" Dani interrupted. There was no way she was letting him keep control of this conversation, not when she didn't know what his purpose was.

Annoyance flashed across his face. "You said you're not opposed to change. I disagree."

"Okay," Dani said slowly. "You're entitled to your opinion. But I don't believe my work performance reflects that." And he'd be hard-pressed to prove it did.

"Oh, Danika." He grinned toothily, and she fought not to cringe away. "You're too caught up on the metrics. Your lack of enthusiasm for change is infecting the office and affecting morale." *What?* "That's why I think you should show everyone that you're on board with the changes we're making here as we evolve into the next phase of the company's development."

Did he realize that he wasn't making sense? And what the hell was he talking about? She should have given in to Ben's puppy eyes and stayed away from work for another day.

"I am on board with keeping this company strong and profitable," she told him flatly. "Figures have been—"

"Danika, Danika, Danika." Seriously, his dumb habit of always using her whole name had never seemed as stupid as it did then. Why add the extra syllable? Nobody called her Danika except her mum when she was in trouble and her siblings and Ben when they were teasing. "You need to let go of the figures. I'm concerned about feelings."

Dani could think of not one thing to say that wouldn't be in breach of employee behavior guidelines, so she kept her mouth shut and waited.

"I want to show the staff that they can feel confident and comfortable about the changes we're making, and the best way to do that is to have management lead by example."

Well, that wasn't wrong… although since when did he give a crap about staff feeling comfortable? He'd tried to cut the break room in half to make way for an "executive dining room," and only gave up on the idea when HR informed him it would be a breach of state law to have a break room that size for the number of employees working on site.

"What did you have in mind?" she asked, feeling as though she were stepping into a trap but unable to see it.

"I'd like you to spearhead our internal job socialization initiative."

Oh, there it is. Hello, trap. Also, what a dumb name.

"And what's that, exactly?" She'd given up on any thought

of being polite. Whatever game Tom was playing now was just to cover his ass. Maybe he was trying to distract her from the debacle of him and Lisa?

"It's a program in which management team members rotate through all the jobs in their departments, demonstrating to staff the standards and job performance expected in each role."

What. The. *Fuck?*

Was he insane?

"That's an interesting idea, Tom," she began, not bothering to keep the contempt out of her voice. "But it's not practical for several reasons." *Not to mention all our managers —except you—have already worked their way up through those roles.*

Tom tsked. He actually *tsked* at her. Dani took a calming breath, then another.

They didn't work.

"Danika, this is what I mean by you being opposed to change. You're unwilling to even consider the idea because it would mean upheaval in your daily routine." The smug look intensified. He thought he had her over a barrel, that she would agree to his asinine scheme in a shortsighted attempt to prove she didn't hate change.

Moron.

"I'm very open to the idea of a program that allows all staff to gain experience from job sharing, and I think a mentorship program, where senior management would demonstrate to employees the skills and abilities they've gained over the years of being in multiple roles, would be an excellent idea. I'm happy to spearhead those initiatives, and will gladly take part in them myself," she countered. "I'm also happy to investigate the logistics of your"—she forced herself not to sneer—"job socialization initiative and do a feasibility study, but I can already see several reasons why it won't work, the first of which is that if you have managers in less senior roles, who will be doing their jobs? Or do you intend to hire new staff?" Surely he didn't believe anyone could be made to do the work of two full-time jobs? They would have WorkSafe breathing down their necks in no time.

"Oh, no," Tom said hastily, no doubt at the idea of spending money on more staff. "That's the beauty of this idea. It dovetails perfectly with the other new program to give staff experience in management roles."

Dani restrained herself from pointing out that having a manager and team member essentially do a job swap was not going to lead to efficient and effective business practices, especially if the team member wasn't properly prepared and qualified. It was also unlikely to engender confidence in the company from their customers. Instead she said, "But that won't work in my department, for example, where the management role is across all sections of the workplace, but each team role is in a different section. None of the administrators has enough experience across all company functions to oversee them. The only cross-function role is the manager." The minute the words were out of her mouth, Dani saw where he was going with this asinine game. Because of course there was one other role in her department that was cross-function: Lisa's. She hadn't counted it because she'd only been considering those jobs that had enough seniority for their incumbents to step into her shoes.

But surely this wasn't all about Lisa? She hadn't expressed any ambition—in fact, she barely seemed to want the job she did have. And Tom was a dickhead and a wanker who didn't have half the business brain his uncle did, but he wasn't so stupid as to believe that an intern with minimal experience and no drive could handle an office manager role for a company of this size—was he?

No, she realized suddenly as he smirked at her. This had

nothing to do with Lisa. Poor Lisa was just the tool he was using, although no doubt he was enjoying whatever they had going on. This was about getting rid of *her*.

He couldn't sack her, so he wanted her to quit.

And the best way to make her quit? Force her to take part in some stupid job swap and give her intern the office manager job. Sure, it was entirely illegal. Her employment contract was for the office manager role. HR would back her up, and if he tried to override them, she could take it to the relevant government body, or to court, and ultimately she would win. He couldn't force her out. She could fight to stay. Her employment record was unblemished. She was popular in the office. Even Harry would be likely to support her—technically the company was still his, even if Tom ran it. In fact, if she went and called Harry now, she could likely put an end to this whole drama.

That weaselly, fuckwit douchenozzle would not win.

But as she sat there, thinking of all the things she could do to steal his victory from him... she realized she didn't want to. She didn't want to continue working in an environment that was becoming more and more toxic by the day. The company she would miss no longer existed. The people... well, she could still see them. Friday night drinks at the pub across the street was open to all, after all. And she could get another job—experienced office managers were in high demand. HR was contractually obliged to give her a reference based on her performance metrics, whether Tom wanted them to or not, and Harry would gladly give her another—he had been her manager for years. She had months' worth of leave days owing to her—she could walk out now, and even if they took four weeks in lieu of notice, they would still need to pay her out the rest. She could go home with Ben for a while, be lazy for a month or so, then start her job search while she was over there and only come back when she was ready for formal interviews.

She would never have to deal with Tom again.

Smiling, Dani met Tom's gaze. His expression changed sharply.

"I resign. Effective immediately. I'll stop by HR on my way back to my office, and as soon as the paperwork is signed, I'll be gone."

At first, he looked confused, as though he couldn't relate her smile to her words. Then that smug look was back.

"If you're sure that's what you want," he said smoothly. "Such a shame that your fear of change is compelling you to make this decision."

For a split second, she considered actually smacking him, but instead she laughed. "Good luck, Tom," she said, and it almost sounded like she meant it.

She walked out of his office feeling lighter than she had for a long time. She didn't even feel guilty about not doing a proper handover. Grinning at Julie, she strolled toward HR, mentally listing the different forms she'd need to complete. At the back of her head, a little voice that sounded suspiciously like her gran was having a celebration, telling her she'd made the right decision.

The folks in HR, with whom she'd worked closely, were shocked and appalled that she was leaving, and for a moment, Dani felt a pang of doubt.

Then she thought of Dickhead Tom's smarmy face and extracted a promise that her termination papers would be ready for her to sign by the time she'd packed up her desk.

As she headed to her office, she pulled out her phone and called Ben.

"Are you calling to finish telling me about Dickhead Tom and the intern?" her bestie demanded.

"No. I'm calling to tell you I'm coming to Monaco."

CHAPTER FOUR

"Do you mean we must *pack boxes?*" Malik heard the incredulity in his own voice as he asked.

Ben and Dani exchanged looks. "Yes?" Ben said, and for some reason it sounded like a question.

Malik turned to Léo. "Why can we not hire someone to do this?"

Dani gasped, and Ben stomped his foot. Léo coughed.

"Er, perhaps this is something best handled ourselves," he said, and then once Ben had humphed in satisfaction and turned away, he shrugged and shook his head with an expression of bewilderment.

Which meant Malik was stuck packing boxes.

Dani and Ben had a clipboard with a list, and they allocated him to a room and told him to pack anything personal. He took that to mean everything in the room and sighed. At least Dani only had a small house. If he took his time, he might be able to get away with doing only this one room.

As thrilled as he was that Dani was coming back to Monaco with them for a long visit, he *did not* like that he'd been designated as a volunteer laborer. Dani apparently had a cousin who was going to stay at her house while she was away, but to quote Dani, "I don't trust her not to sell everything that isn't nailed down," hence the need to pack all personal belongings that Dani might conceivably miss if they went missing. He'd heard mutterings about hiring a van to move the boxes to Dani's parents' garage, but Léo had managed to convince them it was a better idea to get professional movers to do it—thankfully. If he'd had to heave boxes in and out of a truck, he might have caused an irreparable rift in his relationship with his cousin.

Heaving a put-upon sigh that was so impressive, he was sorry nobody had heard it, he taped up a box the way he'd been shown—because Dani and Ben were both such control freaks that they'd had to give a quick lesson on the best way to tape and pack the boxes—and got started with the packing. Surprisingly, it didn't take long to get into a rhythm—probably helped by the fact that he was in the guest room, and since nothing belonged to him, he wasn't distracted by it as he worked. He just put items in boxes.

By the time he'd stripped the surfaces of the dresser and the desk and emptied the desk drawers, he felt… grimy. It was odd, because Dani's house was clean. None of the surfaces he'd touched had been dusty, not even here in a room that clearly didn't get a lot of attention. Yet somehow, he was covered in a film of grime. He went to wash his hands before he tackled the dresser drawers, which he'd been told contained some "extra" clothes.

Half an hour later, he'd successfully dumped the contents of all drawers into boxes. Dani may want to kill him when the time came to unpack, though, because he hadn't been particularly careful. Plus, he seemed to remember she'd said something about lining the clothes boxes with plastic and tissue paper, which he hadn't done.

Well, you got what you paid for.

There was only the wardrobe left, and he was feeling decidedly buoyant when he flung open the doors.

It was, surprisingly, almost empty. Seemingly, Dani reserved this space for formalwear, because there were half a dozen or so cocktail and evening dresses hanging there—he suspected one or two were bridesmaid dresses, because his observations so far had indicated that Dani had good taste, and those dresses were ugly.

Ugly or not, though, he didn't think he should just dump them into boxes, so he went in search of Dani.

It took him only a few minutes to find her in her little shoebox house. "Dani?"

She looked up from taping a box closed. "Hey. You done?"

"Almost," he assured her, hoping he wasn't volunteering himself for extra work. "But do you have garment bags for the dresses in the guest room wardrobe?"

"Oh." She straightened. "I hadn't thought about that. There should be some on the shelf above... or maybe I put them...." She trailed off, pursing her lips, and he resisted the sudden, unwise urge to lean forward and plant a kiss on them. "Let's go look," she suggested finally, and led the way back to the guest room—which seemed absurdly tiny with both of them in there.

Stretching up on tiptoe, she peered at the shelf in the wardrobe. "Yep, they're at the back—I rolled them up and put an elastic band around them to save space, which is dumb because I never put anything else in there. Can you—"

Anticipating her request, he stepped closer and reached past her to the rolled-up cylinders of fabric that were presumably garment bags. They'd somehow ended up right in the back corner, which was why he hadn't seen them before.

"Thanks, Malik—oh!" Dani turned and almost ran into him, presumably because she hadn't realized how close he was. She swayed unsteadily and put a hand on his chest for balance.

Heat exploded through every nerve in his body.

She drew an unsteady breath, tipping her head back to meet his gaze.

The tension between them heightened to almost unbearable levels.

Malik swallowed hard.

And kissed her.

Their lips had barely met when somewhere in the house, Ben shouted, "Dani!" and she jerked back, breathing heavily.

"I…."

"Apologies," Malik managed. "It was… an impulse." Mentally, he kicked himself. Could he have said anything worse?

Nodding, she muttered, "It was that kind of moment. I'd better see what Ben wants." She pushed past him, leaving Malik standing alone in front of her wardrobe with the taste of her on his lips.

MALIK GLANCED over to where Ben and Dani were sleeping curled around each other on one of the plush couches on the private plane, and once more found himself biting back a laugh. He leaned across and nudged Léo.

"What?" His cousin didn't look up from his tablet.

"How can you just pretend they're normal?" he asked, genuinely curious. He adored Ben, of course, and although before this trip he'd only known Dani from anecdotes and group Skype sessions, he would still have said she was a great person. Now, having seen firsthand her strength at her grandmother's funeral, then in dealing with her boss, that had only been reinforced. More, at Ben's insistence they'd made several stops on their way home, spending a few days each in Singapore and Dubai, showing Dani the cosmopolitan cities, and Malik had gotten to know her better. She was fun, more worldly than Ben but just as irreverent. He would gladly count her among his friends—although he supposed technically he already had been, if only by association—and was looking forward to seeing what she made of Monaco. Ben's reactions when he'd first arrived had been memorable.

The kiss… they'd both been pretending it hadn't happened. Malik wasn't sure if that was a good thing or not. Admittedly, it would have been… not right to pursue something now, in these first weeks right after her grandmother's death, when she was grieving and possibly not thinking clearly. But he suspected their aborted kiss was just a precursor of what could happen between them.

In the meantime, he found it just plain odd the way she and Ben finished each other's sentences and curled up like puppies for a nap. They could order for each other in any restaurant too, no matter what kind of food. They had a curious closeness that combined the longtime knowledge and affection of siblings with something that transcended the current societal norm. It was… fascinating.

Léo glanced across at his boyfriend, and his expression softened. "How am I supposed to know what 'normal' is?" he asked. "You and I do not exactly live what most people would call 'normal' lives. This is their normal." He raised an eyebrow at Malik. "What does it matter, anyway?"

Malik sighed. "It doesn't, I suppose." Léo was right—the majority of the population did not consider casual use of a private plane "normal." And Dani and Ben's relationship was sweet, even if he didn't fully understand it.

"Shouldn't you be working?" Léo asked, his attention back on his tablet, where he was reviewing financial reports for some investment he was considering. Malik's eyes darted over to Ben and Dani again, but they were still soundly asleep. "Relax," Léo assured him. "They were up half the night talking about… something. They'll probably sleep the whole way."

Malik considered that. He really did need to do some work, but the last thing he wanted was to answer questions about what he was doing—or worse, have someone catch a glimpse of his laptop screen. But if they were going to be asleep for a few more hours….

He pulled out his laptop and booted it up. Léo glanced over again. "How are your revisions going?" They never, *ever* discussed his work in front of other people—when they were conscious, anyway. Léo was one of fewer than half a dozen people who knew he actually *did* work, much less what he did, and the others were all contractually involved professionals who were obliged to respect his privacy and keep his secret. Not even Lucien knew, which had been difficult for Malik over the years, but he just wasn't ready to share. Certainly his parents didn't know—he could just imagine his father's reaction.

"Fairly well," he told Léo. "I'm not convinced I've got one scene exactly right yet, but I'll get there. There shouldn't be any problem with meeting the deadline."

"Good." Léo nodded, then cast him a sideways glance. "Which scene was that?"

Malik laughed. "I'll send it to you when it's done," he promised. His cousin was his best friend, his brother in all but blood, his staunchest supporter—and his biggest fan. Without Léo, he never would have finished his first book, stuck in the mire of a plot hole, uncertainty and self-doubt overtaking him. Between the two of them and a bottle of whisky, they'd spent a long night hashing out the possibilities, and Malik's natural confidence had reasserted itself.

That book had been taken on by the third agent he sent it to, snapped up by his publisher immediately, and had earned out the modest advance—not that he needed the money—far sooner than anyone had expected. His second book had hit best-seller lists, and things had gotten better since then. He wasn't a list-topper, but his sales were steady and he had a solid fan base.

Most authors would be thrilled by that. For Malik, it was a double-edged sword. He wrote under a pseudonym and viciously guarded his privacy and real identity. Both his agent and editor had initially urged him to publish under his real name, claiming that the publicity they could leverage with it would spur him to instant bestsellerdom, but he'd refused. He already had the press poking into his life; he didn't want to give them more reason to do so. He also didn't want to use an accident of birth to drive sales. He was wealthy because his parents were wealthy (and because Léo was a financial genius), and the resulting party lifestyle in his early-to-mid twenties had made him a recognizable face in the tabloid press, but he wanted to sell books because they were good, not because he'd featured on several eligible bachelor lists and several other "most notorious" lists. That was a naïve and idealistic stand for him to take, but he could afford to, so why shouldn't he? He loved to write and treated it as a career in all other ways, but he would not compromise on keeping his real identity separate from his author self.

It had made some elements of marketing and promotion difficult—he made no appearances, did no public signing events. He did do virtual signings twice a year through several bookstores he'd established relationships with— readers could order signed copies at no additional cost, and Malik would ship the personalized books to the stores. His author social media was mostly run by an assistant at his agent's office—for an additional fee, of course—who also managed his fan mail. He occasionally logged on and posted something, but never anything that could identify him. Fortunately for him, his work didn't attract the kind of rabidly obsessed readers that some other authors had. Most of his readers were happy to enjoy his books and share their feelings in the appropriate forums without being tempted to stalk him or otherwise invade his life.

He got stuck in to his revisions and managed to work through most of the changes he wanted to make before the pilot warned them to strap in for landing. While Léo went to wake the sleeping puppies, he stashed his laptop safely away. By the time Dani and Ben had blinked themselves to consciousness, he was casually playing some inane game on his phone.

"Sleep well?" he asked. Ben stared at him blankly, but Dani nodded.

"Sure. Sleep. Yes. Coffee?"

He and Léo both laughed. "Not right now," Léo said regretfully. "But as soon as we land, we will get you some."

WHEN HE ENTERED HIS APARTMENT, he found it sparkling clean and smelling fresh. This wasn't an unusual occurrence; the concierge ensured that all apartments in the building were visited by the vetted housekeeping service regularly, whether the resident was home or away. It had never before occurred to Malik that many people had to close up their homes when they went abroad and then go through the process of opening them when they returned—at least, not until Ben and Dani had dragged him through the process of packing up Dani's house.

Sighing, he left his luggage by the door and went to pour himself a drink. He'd unpack later; first he wanted to check in with his agent and let her know he'd be back on his normal schedule now and have the revised manuscript to her on time.

Sitting on his balcony, enjoying the warm late-spring air, he waited for the call to connect and then to be put through to Elise.

His agent was a charming but efficient woman in her thirties, and although Malik had been one of her first clients, she now had a list that featured many best-selling authors. He certainly wasn't her most profitable client, but she treated him as though he shat gold. He suspected it had more to do with his personal life and contacts than his books but wasn't above using it to advantage—hence the assistant who managed his social media.

"So," she concluded, having run quickly through the list of changes and dates, "there are no problems, then."

"None at all," he confirmed, his mind already wandering. He wanted to get the last of the changes made this evening so he could tag along over the next few days as Ben and Léo took Dani around Monaco and Nice and the surrounding countryside. Then there was the trip up to Paris planned for next week.

"Well, there is one more thing we need to discuss," Elise said firmly, and his attention snapped back to the call. She only ever used that tone when she had something to tell him that he wasn't going to like.

"Oh?"

"The assistant who looks after your social media is due to go on maternity leave in six weeks and has already advised us that she doesn't wish to return to work. The agency owner has decided that rather than hire a replacement, we will redistribute her confidential work to other assistants, and her other tasks will be undertaken by interns."

His stomach sank. "And there will be nobody who can manage my social media?"

He could almost hear her shrug. "Not consistently, unless we give it to the interns, and given the rotating nature of those jobs, I'm not certain we can trust them not to try to investigate your identity."

He sighed. "Thank you for letting me know—and for taking on the task all these years. What do you suggest?" Because he knew his own limitations, and there was no way he could reliably and consistently post as he should.

"Well...." She hesitated. "You could hire a publicist, but that would likely mean a company and another group of people with potential access to your name. Ideally, you should find an assistant. There are some excellent virtual assistants in the book industry who can manage social media and charge by the hour. Arrange for them to be paid through your lawyer and keep all communication via your author email."

Something in her voice told him she had more on her mind. "But?" he prompted, and she laughed.

"Am I so transparent? So much for my poker face!"

"I'm sure if you wanted to keep secrets from me, you could," he assured her. "But this is obviously something you want to share...?"

"Yes." Her pause spoke volumes. "I think you should consider hiring a full-time assistant."

Malik assimilated that. A full-time assistant?

"I don't need a full-time assistant," he pointed out. Surely managing his social media wasn't a full-time job?

"I disagree. Let me explain why," she said persuasively, and Malik, curious, agreed. "At the moment, your social media presence is minimal. That's purely because we could only allocate so much time to it. If it was expanded, you would likely see a corresponding increase in sales."

"But couldn't a virtual assistant charging by the hour do that for me also? I may be missing something, but even with an expanded social media presence, I don't see it as needing a full-time employee."

"Correct," she agreed. "But if you had a full-time employee with access to an expense account, they could also look at advertising. Your marketing is minimal, much more so than any author should have. You're not interested in doing it for yourself and haven't hired anyone to do it because of the complications in getting people involved with your author persona. I have no doubt that a dedicated advertising campaign and an expanded online presence will send your sales soaring. I know you don't need the money," she pressed on when he tried to interrupt. "But you need to consider the state of the industry. Traditional publishing is under a lot of pressure right now, and a lot of good, solid authors are being dropped in favor of those who can ensure sensational sales numbers. You sell well, but not brilliantly, and if your publisher decides not to offer a contract for your next book in favor of someone who will go the extra mile to market themselves, I don't know that any contract I can get elsewhere will be as good. And since you don't even like to do your own social media, I doubt you'll want to self-publish."

Malik shuddered at the thought. Find his own cover artist? Editor? Copy editor? Proofreader? Have to deal with vendors? Formatting? Marketing? It was bad enough that he was bombarded with questions and requests for information by the people who looked after that—having to do it all himself was just not going to happen.

"No, I don't want to self-publish," he assured her. "So, expand social media and other marketing, and advertise. Is that really a full-time job?"

"No, although when you factor in the time needed to

design the promotional graphics and monitor the ads, the number of hours does creep up. But you could also use your assistant to coordinate the virtual signings—I know you hate how much time that takes. You'd still have to sign the books, of course, but you'll be amazed by how much quicker it will go if you're given a stack that has a Post-it Note with the reader's name on it flagging the title page. They could also do some beta reading for you. Right now, the only person who sees your books before me is your cousin. Another set of eyes is always useful. They could handle a lot of the more time-consuming research and fact-checking. You're meticulous about these things, and we both know it takes a lot of time."

"I like doing the research myself," he pointed out, but his mind was whirling. It would be helpful to have another beta reader—Léo was good, but his perspective was very similar to Malik's, and often the feedback from Elise and his editor was that "most people don't think this way." Since his protagonist was from a background not too dissimilar from Malik's own, he could get away with a lot there, but secondary characters from middle-class or disadvantaged backgrounds sometimes caused him problems. An assistant could also deal with his fan mail. His publisher often forwarded emails that were sent to them, and although he hadn't made his author email address public, it had somehow gotten out there, so his inbox was frequently inundated. Once a week he allocated time to skim over the emails and usually just sent a form "thank you for your email, I'm so glad you enjoy the series" reply, but even that took hours and hours of writing time out of every month.

"I'll consider it," he said abruptly, interrupting Elise's persuasive comments. "I have a few weeks, yes?"

"Possibly a month, but no more," she warned. "You want to allow time for smooth handover of duties."

"Thank you. I will think about this carefully and decide the best way to go forward." He would also do some research into the state of the publishing industry. Because he was so rabid about his privacy, he didn't have much (read: any) contact with other authors. His isolation was by choice, but perhaps he'd done himself a disservice. No contact with others in his industry meant no access to gossip and rumor. And lately he'd been so immersed in writing this book that he hadn't been keeping up with industry journals and blogs. That was poor business sense all around. It was time to open his eyes and make certain he knew what was going on.

CHAPTER FIVE

A week into her stay in Monaco, Dani wondered why she'd waited so long to come. Admittedly, her visit was probably different from the average tourist's. She was staying in a multimillion-dollar apartment (*very* multimillion) and dining at exclusive restaurants. If she'd come with Ben when he first arrived, even with his windfall they wouldn't have been living anywhere near so luxuriously.

Since her arrival, she'd hit all the tourist hot spots, even the ones she had no interest in, at Ben's insistence. Léo and even Malik accompanied them several times, but Dani had quickly learned that an expression of polite interest meant they were deadly bored and had asked if she could have some one-on-one time with Ben. Léo had quickly hidden his relief and graciously acquiesced, going along with the pretense, but Malik had laughed and thanked her.

"When you're done each day with Ben's grand tour of architecture and museums," he'd said, "I'll join you for the parties and restaurants." Ben had pouted for a moment, but the fact was, it was a lot more fun with just the two of them. Dani didn't feel like she had to explain private jokes, for one.

She and Ben often thought along the same wavelength, and others tended to get lost. Plus, although she'd gotten to know Léo, at least, pretty well via Skype over the past year, there still wasn't that ease of manner that develops between close friends. It was coming, she could tell—already she was getting a sense of what Léo and Malik would find funny, things they would enjoy or dislike—but it wasn't quite there yet, and until then, she didn't want to monopolize their time. Truthfully, she also wanted to give them time to get used to her. She knew she could be a bit hard to take sometimes, what with being opinionated, outspoken, and irreverent.

Still, their evenings out, breakfasts at the yacht club, and the glittering parties had been just as much fun as her time exploring with Ben. She'd never eaten so much good food before in her life, and one of the first things she and Ben had done after their arrival was hit the shops, so she had a fabulous new wardrobe of evening wear. They'd carefully negotiated on that—Dani had wanted to pay for her new clothes herself, but Ben had pointedly told her that after she had made him spend a fortune on clothes for himself when he first arrived, he was determined to spend an equal amount on her. That had stumped her—never would she have expected her notoriously tightfisted bestie to willingly spend large sums of cash—but in the end they'd agreed to split the cost fifty-fifty, and Dani would take over cooking duties when they ate at home. So far, it was working well, and she now had some absolutely incredible clothes… that she would probably never wear again once she went home, but she was steadfastly not thinking about that.

Tomorrow, they were going to Paris, and she literally could not wait. Unlike many young Australians, she and Ben had never done the backpacking through Europe thing—nor even a cheap bus tour. They'd both gone straight to uni, where they met, from high school, and although they'd talked several times about deferring for a semester and traveling, in the end it had never happened. Then when they were done with school, "real life" kicked in, and things had never quite lined up for them to travel the globe. They'd managed some overseas trips, but nothing as far as Europe. It had been tremendously hard for Dani to stay behind when Ben had embarked on his European Odyssey, and she knew it had been just as difficult for him to leave her—at one point she'd needed to talk him out of canceling the trip. But she was here now, in amazing Monaco, and tomorrow she was going to Paris. She and Ben had already roughly planned out everywhere else they were going to visit before she had to leave—the list was long, and Dani suspected they wouldn't get through it all, but it would be thrilling to try.

She added a few tops to the bag she was packing, and then went to the wardrobe to decide which of her fabulous evening dresses she would bring. When Lucien had called a few days ago, he'd warned her that his parents were hosting a formal party in her honor—and wasn't that freaky? Léo had assured her that it was basically just an excuse for a party, and all she'd have to do was eat, drink, and mingle, which she would do at any party anyway. He'd added something about a champagne toast, but she wasn't clear on the details of that.

Whatever the party was for, she'd learned that when people here said "formal," they actually meant it. Cute dresses that could transition from office wear to cocktail with the right jewelry and shoes were *not* acceptable. She had several suitable dresses she hadn't worn yet but decided on a royal blue silk dress that clung in all the right places and flowed everywhere else and that Malik had said looked stunning on her.

Not that she was choosing it because of that.

Nope.

She just liked it.

It suited her.

It had cost a fortune, and wearing it only once would be criminal.

Her decision had nothing to do with a clever, funny, unbelievably handsome and wickedly charming man complimenting her.

Dani sighed and sank down on the bed. Who was she kidding? She was totally attracted to Malik and it was screwing with her head.

For starters, despite the compliment and the occasional admiring glance that told her he was definitely aware of her as a woman, he'd never given any indication he wanted to act on that—not since the kiss-that-never-was. Sometimes she almost hated her bestie for interrupting them that day at her house, but in reality, it was probably for the best. They were friends, or rapidly getting there. Dani was on holiday—she had to go back to her real life eventually, and although she wasn't opposed to a holiday fling, there was no way she'd put stress on her friendship with Ben by flinging with his boyfriend's cousin. She knew herself too well—if she was going to embark on a short-term-only relationship, it had to be with someone she was guaranteed to never see again. Otherwise, even if she wasn't interested in more, she would get unwanted feelings of jealousy and possessiveness. It was entirely unreasonable, but that was how she was and why she'd never remained friends with any of her exes. Even though she was happy to have moved on, and thrilled that they had, she was still possessive of them.

So, quite simply, she needed to get past her attraction and focus on being friends with Malik. And that probably meant that she shouldn't be choosing clothes with him in mind. *No to the blue dress*, she decided firmly. She'd pick one of the ones she hadn't worn yet.

A soft knock on the open door had her looking up. Ben stood there, the look on his face far too aware. *Oh, hell.*

"Okay?"

She stood. "Of course. I was just trying to decide which dress to bring to Paris."

"Bring more than one," Ben said, going along with her. "Aside from the Morels', Léo said his sister-in-law is making noises about throwing a party before she gets too pregnant to enjoy it. And bring some of the semiformal outfits, too, for dinner and stuff."

Dani raised her brows. "Stuff? You're so eloquent."

Ben flopped down on the bed and waved a hand. "You know what I mean. Maybe we'll go to the theater or something."

She laughed, and he made a face.

"I know. Who would ever have thought I'd be saying that so casually?"

"You've always liked theater," she argued, but she knew what he meant. Cut-price last-minute seats were different from glittering opening night affairs.

"Anyway," he changed the subject, "Léo's just gone out, and I wanted to talk to you."

Uh-oh. So much for thinking she'd distracted him.

"What about?" *Act casual.*

His level stare was a clear indicator that he saw right through her. She hadn't told him about the kiss, not really, but when she'd gone to see what he wanted that day, she'd been flushed and flustered, and it had taken him only seconds to guess, even if she hadn't confirmed his guess. Since then, he'd had his eagle eye on her.

"It's fine, Ben." He knew her so well; she shouldn't be surprised that he'd seen what she was feeling before she was even willing to admit it to herself.

"Are you sure?" He reached out an arm, and she crawled onto the bed and snuggled next to him.

"Yeah. It's not…. I mean, he's hot, yeah? And he's great. But I'm not in love or anything. It's just attraction, and I can ignore that."

Ben was silent for a second, then he sighed. "I should have considered this." His tone was so filled with blame that she laughed and poked him in the side.

"Don't be an idiot. Not everything is about you, you know. In a week, I'll have forgotten all about this and he'll just be my friend." She rolled off the bed and to her feet. "Come on, I'm hungry. Let's get a snack."

❧

PARIS WAS everything Dani had expected and more. She was surprised by how walkable a city it was—and if she got tired, she could just hop on the Métro. She and Ben had ditched Léo and Malik the first day and gone exploring in typical tourist fashion—well, almost. The tourist crowds were pretty intense even so early in the season, and so Ben had leveraged Léo's influence to get VIP access to the Eiffel Tower. Dani had felt bad about it at first, wanting an "authentic" tourist experience, but when they arrived and she saw how long the lines were, she decided "authentic" was really a matter of perspective. Nothing about this trip was in typical Aussie tourist style, after all, and if she really liked it, she could come back and stand in line another time.

Maybe.

She felt a little less bad about it when they arrived and realized there had been several VIP visits that day, so one of the elevators had been allocated for that purpose, not just for them. They made a brief stop on the second floor, then changed elevators and zoomed up to the third, at the top of the tower. It was such a clear day that Dani felt she could see forever.

"Wow," she said honestly, staring out toward the horizon. "You know, I always thought going up the Eiffel Tower was kind of gimmicky, but this is actually pretty cool."

"I know, right?" Ben slung an arm around her as they wandered slowly around the viewing deck. "While you're here, we should go to Le Jules Verne."

Dani paused to look out over what she was pretty sure was the Bois de Boulogne, if she remembered the map right. "Le Jules Verne? That's the restaurant here in the tower, isn't it? Where Léo brought you for your birthday last year?"

"Yep." He made a face. "Léo doesn't really like it, so I'll have to talk him into it. Or we can just make it the two of us. The view while you're eating... wow."

"That sounds awesome." They walked around for a while longer, taking in the view. Dani could hardly believe that she was actually there, in *Paris*, on the observation deck of the Eiffel Tower. She reached out and touched one of the metal struts, just to make sure it was really there. Ben saw and laughed.

"Come on," he said. "We'll walk down. That will really cement in your brain that it's real."

There were six hundred and something steps down to the ground, and Ben was right—being right in amongst the "guts" of the tower leg was something she'd never forget. Back on the ground, Ben grabbed her hand and dragged her around a corner to... a carousel.

Dani laughed so hard she thought she'd cry while he bought them tickets.

"I can't believe you remembered," she finally gasped as they waited their turn.

He hitched up an eyebrow, smirking smugly. "That you want to ride a carousel in every city you possibly can? Of course I remember. We'd have already started if there was one in Monaco."

Impulsively, she threw her arms around him. "Paris is the perfect place to start."

❧

STEALING a moment to catch her breath, Dani slipped out through a pair of french doors onto a terrace and idly wondered how much wealth one needed to be able to have this much outdoor space in the heart of Paris.

Lucien's parents had a gorgeous home, and they'd treated her like a long-lost daughter. Truthfully, she wasn't sure why. Ben said it was because she'd stepped up to help Lucien and Simon last year, but she hadn't really done much—started an online petition, that's all, and shared it on social media. Sometimes it was the thought that counted, she supposed.

Still, there were worse things than to have a roomful of beautifully dressed people sipping high-end alcohol and eating delicious canapes treat her like a hero. She was dressed to the nines, and even though her feet were killing her in her amazing but impractical shoes, she was having a great time.

"Hiding?"

She started, not needing to turn to know who that deliciously deep voice belonged to. *Damn it!* She wasn't getting over this crush fast enough, and now they were alone together on a moonlit terrace of a Paris mansion. It was goddamn fairy-tale material. How was she supposed to not fall for him under these circumstances?

"Not really," she said finally, shooting him a smile over her shoulder and then returning her attention to the garden as though it was the most fascinating thing she'd ever seen. "Just wanted some air. You?"

He came to stand beside her, and she focused on *not* looking at him with her peripheral vision. "I saw you come out and wanted to ensure you were not overwhelmed."

This time she turned to look at him properly. "Overwhelmed?" The incredulity in her voice spoke volumes. Her, overwhelmed at a party? Sure, he didn't know her well, but did he know her *at all*?

He laughed. Hard. In fact, were those tears streaming down his face? "Forgive me," he gasped, swiping at his eyes. "I could not resist." He grinned at her. "You should have seen your face. The very thought of being overwhelmed was anathema to you."

She couldn't help it: she laughed too. "It really is," she agreed. "It's probably not healthy, but I've spent so long being capable and competent that I can't stand the idea of anything else." She smiled up at him. At five seven, she wasn't exactly short, and the four-inch stiletto heels she was wearing added to that, but he was still taller. Was it wrong that she found that incredibly sexy? And he looked divine in his formal evening clothes. Something fluttered in her stomach.

Damn, damn, damn.

"You don't look capable and competent tonight," he said, his voice dropping an octave.

Oh. My. God. Was he flirting with her?

"You look… sensational." He leaned in close enough that she could feel the warmth from his body.

He is. He's flirting with me. How seriously should she take this? Was it casual flirting between friends, or was there *intent*? And how was she supposed to work it out when her skin was flushing hot and every nerve ending in her body was tingling?

"Thank you," she said, and yay for her, there was no shakiness or breathiness in her voice at all. But she had no idea what to say next. "You look pretty sensational yourself."

Shoot me. It was like she'd never flirted before. Why was it that when you actually liked someone, all skill at flirting disappeared?

He grinned again, and regret rushed through her. Just friendly, then. "Come back inside," he said, slinging an arm around her shoulders in much the same way Ben would. Definitely just friends. "They're going to serve dessert soon, and Lucien's mother favors the most incredible patisserie. I've been waiting for this all night."

Swallowing her disappointment and chiding herself for feeling it in the first place, she smiled. Dessert was something she could get behind. "Find me another glass of champagne, and I'm in."

"Consider it done."

CHAPTER SIX

alik assured himself that things were better this way. If Dani had flirted back with him, he would have taken it further, and that would have been foolish. Getting sexually involved with a friend was complicated, and often a bad idea. And they *were* friends now.

But it would be so good.

Maybe, but was he willing to risk causing awkwardness later? He and Dani didn't know each other very well yet, but he and Léo were closer than brothers—certainly closer than he was to his actual brothers—and Ben was a permanent part of Léo's life, which meant Dani would be in their lives forever too. Even though she lived in Australia, the number of Skype calls he'd been included on in the past was an indication that he'd be seeing a lot of her in the future.

But... you saw her in that dress....

Fixing his smile in place, Malik shifted in an attempt to adjust himself without actually having to adjust himself in a room full of people—including his aunt and uncle, who were bearing down on them. Now was not the time to think about how delectable Dani looked in that dress.

But did it have to be scarlet? He had a weakness for a beautiful woman in a red dress.

"Malik!" His aunt swooped in and presented her cheek. Dutifully, he kissed it and then shook his uncle's hand.

"Aunt Miryam, Uncle Charles. Are you enjoying the evening?"

Dani stepped forward to perform her own greetings. Léo and Ben had introduced her earlier in the week when they went for their duty dinner. Malik had begged off; it wasn't that he didn't love his aunt and uncle—they had, after all, practically raised him—but his aunt and mother had been conspiring for some time now to get him married and settled, and he wanted to avoid the battle of words and wits that entailed. Especially since his father had been calling lately and he'd been dodging the calls.

"Vivienne and Édouard always throw such lovely parties," Aunt Miryam said dismissively, as though she expected nothing less. "Have you been here all evening, Malik? We haven't seen you."

Possibly because I've been ducking out of sight every time you come into view. "I've been circulating," he prevaricated. "We have probably been missing each other by moments."

"Most likely," Charles agreed, with a particular gleam in his eye that told Malik he wasn't buying it for even an instant. "There are so many people here. How are you enjoying Paris, Danika?"

Malik was standing close enough to Dani to feel her almost imperceptible flinch at the use of her full name, but she smiled and answered warmly.

"It's wonderful. I wish I'd let Ben talk me into coming sooner, and I'm so looking forward to seeing more."

For a few minutes, they spoke politely about the sights Dani had seen and the places she should try to see while she was in Europe. Malik was beginning to think he might be able to get away without any personal conversation; Aunt Miryam was a stickler for formal, old-fashioned social etiquette and wouldn't spend more than ten minutes at a time with any person or group of people at a party. But just as they reached what he estimated was the eight-minute mark, the Europe chatter wound down and Aunt Miryam turned to him.

"I spoke with your mother yesterday," she said. "Have you heard from her lately?" The question sounded innocent enough to any observer, Dani included, but it was actually pointed. He made a duty call to his mother at least once a fortnight and spent that time dodging questions and lectures about his life. It used to be every Monday morning, but his father had started hijacking the conversations, and so now the calls were less frequent and he tried to make the time and day random.

"Last week," he said casually, as though the call hadn't ended with his father grabbing the phone, a shouting match, and then Malik stomping around his apartment slamming doors. "She sounded well then. Excited about the wedding." His youngest sister, who at nineteen was barely old enough to think for herself if you asked him, was getting married soon. He was still trying to come up with an excuse not to go to the wedding, although there was no way he could do that without breaking his sister's heart.

"She is," Miryam agreed. "She said your father has been trying to call, but he doesn't seem able to catch you."

And there it was. She wasn't pulling any punches, meeting his gaze squarely. His mother and Aunt Miryam were twins, and although he'd often gotten the feeling that she didn't like his father, his aunt was *always* on his mother's side. No matter what. And since his mother was almost always on his father's side—the only exception Malik could think of was when she decided to send him to France for his schooling—that meant Aunt Miryam would nag him about taking his father's calls.

"I noticed I'd missed him a few times, but never at a convenient time to call back." He smiled. It was his social smile, not a real one, and he knew his aunt had noticed when she drew back slightly.

Rescue came from a totally unexpected direction.

"I'm sure you'll find time sooner or later," Uncle Charles said dismissively. "If it were urgent, he would have tried to reach us. My dear, we should speak with Guy and Lauren." He gave Miryam no time to protest, turning to Dani and telling her how nice it was to see her again and that she should be sure to call on them again before returning to Australia. Aunt Miryam was left with no option but to reiterate his invitation, and then he swept her away.

Malik forced himself not to sag in relief.

"Wow," Dani said. "That was intense. Do you want to sneak back outside for a bit?"

Should he be charmed or feel awkward and embarrassed that a woman he was halfway to infatuated with had just witnessed him squirming because his aunt told him to call his father?

Dani met his gaze solidly, no pity visible, no curiosity or salacious interest.

"No, but thank you. I apologize if we made you uncomfortable with our family drama."

She laughed. "It would take more than a few casual words spoken politely to make me uncomfortable," she told him, sliding her arm through his and tugging him toward a window as though she'd done it a thousand times before. "Remind me sometime to tell you about the first time my brother ever brought a girlfriend to a family Christmas, and two of my cousins had a screaming fight at the lunch table and stormed out. A lot of dirty laundry got aired that day." With her free hand, she scooped a champagne glass from the tray of a passing waiter, handed it to him, and then liberated another for herself. By the time they reached the window niche, he was chuckling along with her story, sipping from his glass, and generally enjoying the sensation of her beside him. Too bad he was wearing a tuxedo—her hand on his arm would be so much better skin-to-skin.

"Thank you," he murmured when she paused. "It's very kind of you to look after me."

She winced. "I hope you don't think I'm being... I don't know, patronizing or anything."

"Not at all," he assured. "I think you know me better than I thought you did."

Glancing away, Dani murmured, "Yeah, I figured you wouldn't want anyone seeing you... not being you."

Ah. Malik lifted his glass and sipped, buying himself a second. She was far more intuitive than he'd given her credit for, something that was reinforced when he lowered his glass and saw the knowing smirk on her lips. He couldn't quite bite back his grin.

"Very good," he acknowledged. "Aunt Miryam is likely the only person who could do that to me in a public setting, and usually only when the topic is my father." He decided to go for broke; if she was going to be around for a while, she would likely overhear quite a bit about his family situation. "Has Ben told you about my father?"

She shrugged. "Only that you and he don't get along that well."

That was an understatement and surprised him a little. "I thought you and Ben told each other everything."

Her shrug this time was a little rueful, acknowledging

that she knew she and Ben shared more than most people thought was normal. "Not other people's secrets."

From the corner of his eye, he saw the waitstaff begin circulating with the dessert trays, and he took Dani's arm and pulled her a little further back into the room. "They're bringing around the pastries and I don't want them to miss us," he explained when she raised a brow inquiringly. Instantly, she looked around.

"Can you tell what's on the trays?" She squinted toward one of the waiters, and Malik smothered a laugh.

"Not from here, but they'll get to us." A warm feeling spread through his chest as he looked down at her. He was *this close* to just throwing logic and reason out the window and making a move on her—a real one, one she couldn't pretend was something else.

She turned back and met his gaze, and color rose on her cheeks. Perhaps he wasn't as discreet as he'd thought. For a long, frozen moment, their gazes held. Malik's chest was tight. He should go for it. He should—

"Why are you two hiding over here?"

The room snapped back to life, and air filled his lungs as the moment passed. Dani smiled at Lucien, and if it was a little shaky, it wasn't so obvious that he noticed.

"We're not—" she began.

"We were hiding from Aunt Miryam," Malik interrupted bluntly, and winked at her. "And now we're waiting for dessert."

Lucien chuckled. "Both completely understandable endeavors," he said blandly. "Are you still dodging your father?"

Malik nodded and left it at that. Lucien had been a friend for long enough to know everything—*almost* everything about him. As usual, he felt a pang of guilt for keeping such a big secret as his writing career from his friend, but still, something prevented him from sharing.

Making his guilt even worse, Lucien didn't press him about his father. Instead, he looked around and then said, "Why don't we sneak away? I'll send word to the kitchen and have a tray sent to one of the sitting rooms for us, and then I'll round up Si and Léo and Ben. We can have dessert in private."

"Will your parents mind?" Dani asked, but Malik could see how much the idea appealed to her. It certainly appealed to him.

"Not at all. It's possible nobody will even notice we're gone, but we'll slip back in before people start leaving."

She looked up at him. "It would certainly help us to stay out of your aunt's way."

Us. Pushing down the urge to whisk her behind one of the window draperies and kiss her senseless, he replied, "It would. Thank you, Lucien, that sounds wonderful."

In short order, he and Dani were strolling nonchalantly out of the room, headed for the upstairs family parlor, while Lucien went to liberate some dessert and the rest of their friends.

DANI JOLTED AWAKE—LITERALLY. Someone had leaped onto her bed, sending her bouncing. She was an intelligent woman, but it didn't take much brains to work out who was responsible for her rude awakening.

"Ben, get off! What the hell is wrong with you?" She pulled the sheet up over her head and buried herself in the pillow. She had no idea which manufacturer made the beds in Léo's apartments, but she highly recommended them.

"Nope! We gotta talk," Ben insisted, ripping away the

sheet—her protective shield. She hissed and swiped a hand in his direction, but the annoyingly cheerful bastard leaned back out of reach.

"Since when are you a morning person?" she groaned. "I'm on holiday, for God's sake. Let me sleep in."

The bed bounced again as he flopped down to lie beside her. "You can go back to sleep in a bit," he promised. "Léo's gone out, and we need to talk before he gets back."

Huffing, she rolled onto her back and turned her head to look at him. "Why do we need to talk while he's out? Are we keeping secrets from him?" Suddenly wide awake, she sat up and studied him with concern. "Is everything okay?"

Ben sat up too and arranged the pillows so he could prop himself against the headboard. He was still in the torn T-shirt and flannel pants he slept in. "It's all good with me and Léo," he assured her.

Sighing in relief, she leaned against the pillows. "So why are we talking while he's out?" she asked, resigned to the fact that she was awake and unlikely to fall back asleep.

"Because I don't think he knows there's something going on between you and Malik."

Oh.

Well, crap.

"There's nothing going on between me and Malik," she protested. It was even the truth—sort of.

Ben raised an eyebrow, his expression one of pure disbelief. "You forget, Dani, I was there last night."

"Nothing happened last night," she insisted. Damn him and his best friend intuition. "Maybe I wanted it to, but it didn't."

"Did he want it to?"

Dani rubbed her forehead. "You're asking all the hard questions. I don't know. I think maybe he did, but it's not like we talked about it. And nothing happened, so…. Really, Ben, you're blowing this out of proportion. I'd never do anything to cause problems for you here." It actually kind of hurt a bit that he thought she might. She'd understood his initial concern, but for him to keep harping on it….

She looked up and caught sight of the astonishment on his face. "Is that what you think? That I'm worried something between you and Malik might be a problem for me?"

Er… how was she supposed to respond?

"Well… yes. Ow!" She rubbed her upper arm where he'd pinched her. "Don't be violent!" It freaking hurt—he'd always been good at pinching.

"That was for thinking I'd care more about a hypothetical problem for myself than about you doing something fun that made you happy." They both winced as they realized how that sounded. "You know what I mean."

"I know," she agreed, although it was true that doing Malik would likely be fun and make her happy. "I'd apologize, but I still don't know what this is *about*."

Rolling his eyes, he said, "I'm trying to matchmake, you doof. You and Malik are two of my favorite people in the world, and you'd be *perfect* together."

It was like a punch to the solar plexus. For a moment, Dani just sat there, stunned, unable to react. Then her brain came back online.

"Oh, Ben, that's…." *Fuck.* Pretty much the only thing holding her back from making a move on Malik had been concern for Ben's future, and here he was basically giving her permission—hell, encouraging her. But… it didn't change the fact that if things didn't work out, it could get really awkward.

She said as much to Ben, who scoffed. "Were you not listening to me a second ago? You two are perfect for each other. This isn't something that just occurred to me, Dani— I've been thinking about it for over a year. I just needed to see you together to make sure my instincts were right—and they are."

It really sank in then that Ben meant to play matchmaker, and panic rose. "Don't meddle," she warned, trying to sound casual. "If things progress, it will be because Malik and I both want it and are ready, *not* because of some stupid *Parent Trap*-style plot you hatched up in that half-grown brain of yours."

Ben sniffed in mock offense and then smacked her in the face with a pillow. "Fine," he declared as she clawed it away. "I won't interfere—yet."

That didn't make her feel any better.

IN WHAT SEEMED an incredible stroke of fate, later that day the manager of one of Léo's estates (because he actually had *estates*, plural) called to advise of some issue with irrigation or broken pipes or something—Ben hadn't cared enough about the details to ask for them. After a lengthy phone conversation, Léo decided he needed to go out there. That struck Dani as decidedly weird—wasn't he supposed to be a billionaire dilettante? Sure, he was a financial wizard, but most people didn't know that, and most financial advisors weren't experts in fixing broken pipes or irrigation or whatever. When she said as much to Ben, he just shrugged.

"Mostly I think he's going because it makes the people working on the estate feel better," he offered. "He can stride around being all Mr. Important Master of the Manor or whatever, and they'll breathe easier because the fact that he came all that way means he actually gives a shit about the property and they're not going to lose their jobs."

Huh.

"How very insightful of you," she mocked, chopping peppers. He threw a dishcloth at her. "Are you going with him?" *Please say no.* If Ben went, she'd feel obliged to go too, and although she was sure the Swiss countryside where the property was located was gorgeous, she had too much to see in Europe to disappear off to the backwoods.

Ben shook his head. "No. You and I are going to Italy, and Malik is going with Léo."

Her heart thumped harder. "Oh." She couldn't think of a reason to ask why Malik was going, and that made her feel stupid, especially since Ben already knew she had a thing for Malik.

Luckily, her bestie knew her too well and volunteered the information. "Apparently phone reception is a bit spotty on this property, so if Malik goes with Léo, he has a legit reason for dodging his dad's calls."

Dani put down the knife and turned to Ben. "What's up with that? It came up last night, too—Miryam made a big song and dance about it. Well…" She made a face. "Not a song and dance like we would, but in her way."

Sighing, Ben snitched a piece of pepper. "It's complicated. Malik's sister is getting married, yeah? And he's expected to go home for the wedding. He doesn't go back much, but always for big family things, especially when Léo and Charles and Miryam and Gabriel are invited too."

"Right. That makes sense." Although it was kind of sad that he needed a buffer to visit his family.

"So, Léo's always been out, right, but he's never really been public about it. He's dated, but not anyone that the paps cared about, so it was always one of those things that everyone knew but nobody really thought about."

Dani winced. She could see where this was going, and she didn't like it.

"Then he met me, and I moved in with him, and the paps don't care about me, but he's not just dating me; we're living together. Invitations to social events have to include me—

it's unforgivably rude if they don't. So the wedding invite has my name on it… but then Malik's dad, who could ignore Léo being gay when it was a non-issue but is actually a raging homophobe as well as just a general asshole, called Malik and told him he had to convince us to decline the invitation."

Yep. She didn't like it.

"What a fucking wanker."

Ben nodded. "Pretty much. So Malik told Léo that he expects us to be at the wedding or he's not going. Léo told him not to be an idiot, because his sister, who's really sweet, would be devastated if he wasn't there, but if Léo and I go, there's every likelihood that at some point there will be an ugly scene—"

"Which would upset the bride," Dani concluded with a sigh. "Benji, this sucks."

"Yep. They argued about it for a while, and so far no decision has been made, but we need to RSVP soon. In the meantime, Malik's dad has been hounding him about it, and probably will until Léo and I decline the invitation."

"You're definitely going to decline?"

It was Ben's turn to sigh. "I don't know what other option we have," he admitted. "Aside from not wanting to ruin the wedding and upset the bride, I'm not really keen to go somewhere I'm not wanted, where at least one person will be openly hostile. I suggested to Léo that he should go without me, but he refuses to consider it. He's really pissed about this whole thing but trying not to let Malik see—which is dumb, because Malik knows him better than anyone, and he knows."

"So the problem is, how do you decline but still get Malik to go? I'll bet the more douchey his dad is, the more he doesn't want to go."

"That's it in a nutshell. I'm hoping Léo will convince him

while they're gone, because we'll definitely need to RSVP by the time they get back."

Dani thought about that for a moment, remembering the carefully blank look on Malik's face when his aunt had nagged him about returning his dad's calls. "Let's open a bottle of wine."

CHAPTER SEVEN

Glaring at his laptop screen, Malik damned social media to hell. Oh, it was all fine to use on a casual, communicate-with-friends basis, but from a business promotional perspective… it was the devil's work, and there was no way he'd manage it himself.

Not that he'd been seriously considering it. Maybe the thought had crossed his mind, because he'd been procrastinating on the whole assistant decision and if he took over his own social media, the need for that decision would cease to exist. But then he'd have to manage his own social media, and since he hated all the administrative tasks he was already handling, it seemed stupid to add something as monolithic as social media management to them.

Which left him right where he'd been an hour and a half ago, before he'd begun looking at the online presence of other authors. Should he hire a PR firm or an assistant?

Heaving a sigh, he closed the lid of the laptop.

"Problem?" Léo asked as he came into the snug little parlor Malik had been using as an office.

"Not really," he replied, shaking his head, then changed

his mind and nodded. "Actually, yes. You have an assistant. What's it like?" He couldn't believe he'd overlooked this before. Léo was the perfect person to ask for advice.

His cousin paused halfway between standing and sitting before settling on the leather Chesterfield in front of the window. "What's it like? It's like… having an assistant."

Malik shot him a dirty look as he stood from the elegant writing desk and joined him on the couch.

"Perhaps if you tell me what you want to know, I can help more," Léo offered in a conciliatory tone, even as his expression told Malik he was being laughed at.

He sighed again, letting his head drop back against the back of the couch. "There's going to be a reshuffle at my agent's office, and they won't be able to manage my social media anymore," he explained. "My agent thinks that instead of hiring a PR firm, I should get an assistant and have them take over more of the administrative duties so I can just write." He repeated her comments on the state of the industry and told Léo about the information he'd found that backed it up. "Eventually, I may want to self-publish," he admitted. It was a conclusion he'd come to after hours of research, and one he didn't particularly like. "I'm in a good position for it, with an established readership and no concerns about income or cashflow. But there would be a lot more admin involved in that, and it would take time I don't want to spend." Malik was nothing if not honest with himself about his faults. He knew his weaknesses, and there would be no point in committing himself to something that ultimately he wouldn't want to follow through on. Being financially independent meant that he would feel no pressure to continue publishing if it was no longer enjoyable to him— and although he did get a certain satisfaction from being published, it was writing that he truly loved. His financial position meant he could spend all his days writing as a hobby without ever needing to publish.

His ego, on the other hand, did not like that idea, and neither did his business brain. They both urged him to ensure he was successful and productive in all his endeavors.

"It sounds as though an assistant is the right choice," Léo said thoughtfully, his brows drawn as he considered all aspects of the issue. "You would need to set things in place to ensure your privacy remains intact, but ultimately, it's a good idea. Why do you dislike it so?"

"I don't know," Malik admitted, trying not to pout like a child. "Logically I can see that it's the step I need to take, but… I suppose I've never employed anyone directly before. It's always been firms and agencies and management companies."

Léo frowned. "Neither have I," he said, in the tone of someone making an unusual discovery. "In fact, Jean is assigned to me by an agency. So there you go. You won't need to employ your assistant directly, either."

They looked at each other silently for a long moment.

"Are you thinking that you now want to employ someone directly?" Malik asked finally, and Léo laughed.

"Yes. It seems wrong that I pay the salaries of so many people, but none of them actually work for me on paper."

"Good." It was a relief not to be the only one with such foolish thoughts. "We can both take on the challenge of being employers. You first, so I can learn from your mistakes."

Léo's scathing look didn't dent his sudden good mood.

"How are things with the new irrigation system?" he asked, gesturing vaguely toward the window that showed beautiful, if bucolic, scenery. He didn't really care that much, but Léo had spent an hour cursing several evenings earlier as he attempted to learn the ins and outs of irrigation, and he liked riling his cousin.

Unfortunately, Léo merely smiled. "The installation is going well, and the manager seems much more comfortable. In a day or so, he should be confident enough for us to leave."

"There's no rush," Malik assured him. "I'm getting a lot of writing done, and it's nice not to have the phone ringing." Not satisfied with Léo's promise of intermittent reception, he'd just turned the thing off after sending a message to his mother that he was going to be in a remote area and probably noncontactable.

"On that topic," Léo began, and Malik wished he'd kept his mouth shut. Damn, damn, damn. "Ben asked me to speak to you about the wedding."

"*Ben* asked you?" he sniped. "Leaping to do his bidding, are you?" He felt ashamed of himself for saying it even before Léo shot him a level look.

"*Ben* asked me to speak to you about the wedding because he's worried about you," Léo continued calmly. "He doesn't want to put you in a position where you feel obliged to make a stand on our behalf, and he doesn't want you to be unhappy. Tell me, Malik, if your father were not a part of this decision at all, how would you feel to miss Houria's wedding?"

Malik clenched his jaw and swallowed hard. Léo always knew exactly where to hit. "Unfortunately, my father *is* a part of this decision—and that's of his own choosing." His father had always been a hard man, set in his ways and determined that his children would measure up to his standards. It was no secret that Aunt Miryam's request for Malik to move to France to be company for Léo had been a slim cover for his own mother's desperation to get him away from his father. Not that his father was physically abusive, but Malik had been an inquisitive, active child. He remembered often asking "why" and "how" and wanting to see for himself, and his father, who was of the opinion that children were to be seen upon request, not heard, and always obedient, had responded with harsh words and punishments. Being confined to his bedroom, as luxurious as it was, had been agony to young Malik. More, his enthusiasm and curiosity had engendered an attitude of almost dislike from his father, and Malik had become resentful when his siblings had received praise for things he was also doing, but he had not.

Worst of all had been that everyone in the household noticed. The tension between the adult male and his by then six-year-old son had been palpable, and his mother had begged her sister for help finding a solution. So Malik had moved to France to be raised with his cousin and receive a European education—which would ostensibly assist when he took his place in his father's business.

But for all his father's hardheadedness, he loved his family and firmly believed in the concept of it. That was what hurt so much right now. Not just that he was willing to essentially uninvite his nephew from a family event, but that he was putting Malik in such a difficult position. The world knew that Léo was not just his cousin, but his best friend—like a brother to him, in many ways more than his actual brothers. How could his father expect him to be the tool of such a blow?

"If he had any respect for family, for the fact that this should be a joyous day for Houria, he would never have even dreamed of asking this of me," Malik insisted. "He would welcome you and Ben. Houria and Ben have connected on social media—how will she feel if you and he don't come to her wedding? Father hasn't stopped to consider anyone's feelings but his own, and his own are petty, homophobic, and a disgrace to our family." He stopped and took a deep breath. He'd known how angry he was about the situation, of course, but the habit he'd formed of dodging his father's calls had morphed into dodging all thoughts and conversations about the wedding. Ranting about it felt... good. He was still angry, still felt frustrated and impotent over the whole issue, but putting his feelings into words had eased some of the pressure on his chest.

"Yes," Léo said quietly. "It pains me to say it, but Uncle's actions disappoint us all. He and I have never been close, you know, but it... it still hurts, what he's doing. Part of me wants to bring Ben to the wedding and every party and gathering before and after, to hold his hand and kiss him in public and flaunt our relationship as loudly and crassly as possible. It would serve him right, yes?"

Yes! But even as part of him surged triumphantly at the idea of rubbing his father's face in his own prejudice, he knew that could never happen. It wasn't fair to his sister, who was so excited about her wedding. It wasn't fair to Ben, to drag him into a hostile family situation. And it wasn't fair to Léo, who had never been publicly demonstrative. It wouldn't change anything, either, and after the initial satisfaction, there would probably be a series of confrontations, awkwardness, and all manner of other problems to deal with.

In the end, nobody would win, and everybody would be miserable.

"It's not right," he said, a last-ditch protest, but they both knew he'd conceded the point.

"I know."

They sat in silence for long moments. Malik struggled with his decision—he wanted to see Houria married, but going without Léo didn't just feel like conceding a victory to his father, it would also leave him without a buffer. His father would be busy playing host for most of the week, but he would find time to tell Malik—in detail—what a disappointment he was. And his brothers.... One was a decent man, although they had little in common, but the other was a shadow of their father and could only be tolerated in short stints within groups.

"I'll be thirty-one soon," he said finally. "I suppose I should learn to deal with my family without needing a bodyguard."

Léo snorted. "You've never needed a bodyguard," he corrected. "The problem has never been that you're afraid to deal with them, it's that you don't want to offend them. You're so worried about damaging the already tenuous relationship you already have that you avoid speaking to them about anything important—and the best way to do that is to always have someone with you."

Malik felt like he'd been punched. He'd never thought of it that way, but Léo was right. It was so much easier to keep contact between him and his family light—to avoid anything important for fear it might lead to questions like *how could you just let me go* and *why don't you love me like you do the others*. He loved his life, and he'd loved growing up in France with Léo as his constant companion. If given the chance to go back and change things, he wouldn't. But that didn't mean part of him didn't still wonder how his parents had so easily parted with him. After he'd moved to France, he'd seen his family on average perhaps twice a year. Given their wealth, that was an astoundingly low incidence. As an adult, he much preferred to maintain an easygoing and irregular contact with his sisters and tolerable brother, with a regular duty call to his mother, than to institute a closer relationship with any of them and discover that the reason for such distance during his childhood had been down to him.

Or worse—if he built closer ties with his siblings now, he may be subjected to reminiscences of the family time he hadn't been a part of. Uncle Charles and Aunt Miryam had treated him as their own, and he had his own trove of "family" memories… but it wasn't really the same.

He sucked in a deep breath. Léo was right, but he was also wrong. It wasn't fear of damaging existing relationships that compelled Malik to bring a buffer along when he went back to Saudi Arabia—or at least, not just that. He feared *any* change to those relationships, anything that might drag up his emotional insecurities.

But he'd never say so out loud. It was bad enough he'd just admitted it to himself.

"I suppose I'll just have to practice my diplomacy, then," he replied to Léo. "I won't let Houria down by not attending her wedding." The moment he said the words, a weight lifted from his chest. It was immediately replaced by the weight of dread, but at least he knew he'd made the right decision. "And you and Ben can have a barrel of scotch waiting for me when I get back." Because it would be wrong for him to insist that Léo and Ben be subjected to his father's hate.

"We will," Léo said gravely, then, "Thank you."

Malik huffed a sigh, then snorted a laugh. "Okay, I think I'm done with the melodrama for now." He heaved himself up from the Chesterfield and strolled over to the cabinet where Léo kept the alcohol. "Too early for a drink?" he asked by rote, selecting a bottle of Lillet.

"It's afternoon," Léo said, "and we've just waded through heavy personal issues. I think a drink is appropriate."

Malik glanced back over his shoulder. "And if we hadn't?"

His cousin grinned at him. "It's afternoon, isn't it?" A moment later, he accepted the glass Malik handed him. "You know, you won't be completely without a shield at the wedding," he commented. "My parents are attending—and Gabriel and Celine."

"True," Malik conceded, and took a sip from his glass. "And as I recall, Celine was quite offended when she heard you and Ben weren't going to be welcome."

"She was," Léo agreed. "She would never dream of causing

a scene, but she's exquisitely gifted at impeccably polite snubs."

Sinking back onto the couch, Malik smiled. His father would never disgrace himself by insulting a female relative, especially if her behavior was within the boundaries of socially acceptable. Perhaps this wedding wouldn't be so bad, after all.

❦

DANI FLOPPED down on her bed in Léo and Ben's Monaco apartment, thinking that it was good to be home—and wasn't that a trip, that she was thinking of Monaco as home? Still, it was her base of operations for her European travels, so it made sense.

The last few weeks had been frantically busy, but amazing. She got it now, why so many young Aussies spent time working in Europe. It was a completely different life experience to Australia. She was rather tempted to look into getting a job here herself and sticking around, but....

But what? Again she reminded herself that there was no pressing reason for her to go back to Australia anytime soon. Sure, she'd miss her family, but it wasn't like she'd never see them again—they could Skype or FaceTime regularly. She'd probably end up talking to them more than usual. Her little house wouldn't really be an issue either—her cousin had been talking about how great it was to be out of home and could probably be talked into renting the place from her.

Ben knocked once on the doorframe and then came in and dropped onto the bed beside her. "Happy to be back?"

She rolled her head to the side and grinned at him. "Yep. It's been amazing, but I'm ready for some lazy days."

"Lazy days are the best," he mumbled, eyes closed, and Dani chuckled. He could say whatever he wanted, but give him more than a few days of inactivity and he would be climbing the walls. They were the same in that respect.

"I'm surprised you're not still cuddling with Léo," she said idly, and he waved a hand.

"He had to take a call." Léo had returned to Monaco the day before, which Dani thought was suspiciously convenient timing—he was back in good time to see Ben but didn't have to join them on their tourist explorations. When she'd said as much to Ben, he'd given her a bland look and asked if she was surprised.

"How'd it go at the estate?" She hadn't bothered to ask when she'd greeted Léo upon arrival, choosing instead to go to her room as soon as possible to give him and Ben time together.

Ben sighed and rolled to his side, opening his eyes. "Fine, I guess. If there was a real problem, he'd still be there." He propped himself up on an elbow and narrowed his gaze. "You're plotting something."

Damn that best friend intuition. "Not really," Dani hedged, but his disbelieving glare was immediate. "Well, not plotting, exactly. I was just considering getting a job and living in Europe for a year or two."

Ben sat up so fast he nearly fell off the bed. "Yes! Definitely, you should do that. I'll help you look!" He was on his feet and halfway to the door before she could blink.

"Benji, wait! I'm only thinking about it right now." The words were no sooner out of her mouth than she realized how ridiculous they were.

He paused. "Why? What's holding you back?" The challenge in his tone was highlighted by an annoyingly raised eyebrow. She wanted to yank it off his face. Were all best friends so irritating?

Defensive, much? The only time she really, truly found Ben annoying was when he was right about something.

She sighed. "Nothing, I guess," she admitted, and his face lit up.

"Yesssssss! Come on, let's go call an employment agency," he urged. "The one that finds me nursing work has other departments."

Dani bit her lip. "Actually, I was thinking I'd probably settle in Paris or London," she ventured.

And the battle began.

❧

MALIK RANG the doorbell perfunctorily and then let himself into Léo and Ben's apartment. He'd been assured many times that he was welcome to use his key whenever and come and go as he pleased, but he always rang the bell to give warning. Several times he'd been greeted by Léo's shout to wait in the living room—once, to wait at the café down the street. He still teased them both about that one.

This time, he was met with shouting—but it wasn't Léo and wasn't aimed at him. In fact, his cousin stood in the entrance hall, clearly listening to the, er, *enthusiastic* conversation in the living room but making no move to join it. Malik closed the door and went to join him.

"What is it?" He kept his voice low, but Léo still raised a finger to his lips.

"They've been arguing for an hour, at least," he murmured, and Malik felt a stab of admiration. It took real dedication and stubbornness to maintain a shouting fight for that long. He nearly asked Léo what they were arguing about but decided to listen instead.

"—so stupid you make my teeth ache! This has nothing to do with you—I'm trying to be practical. How many times do I need to tell you? Should I use small words or speak slowly so you'll understand?" That was Dani, screeching.

"Hah! Don't bother—I don't need to hear you make crap up. All you need to say is that you don't want to be here, Dani—treat me with at least that much respect!" Ben, injecting every ounce of melodrama he could harness into his words. Malik nearly burst into tears from his tragic tone alone.

"This. Is. Not. About. YOU!"

"EVERYTHING is about me!"

Silence.

Then they both burst into hysterical laughter. Malik shot Léo a glance and found his confusion mirrored on his cousin's face.

"Everything is about you?" Dani sounded like she might be crying from laughter. Ben was gasping for breath, not even bothering to answer.

Léo raised a brow at Malik and tipped his head toward the door, and Malik nodded. He was willing to take the risk to find out what was going on.

In the living room, Ben and Dani were sprawled haphazardly on the couch, tears streaming down their faces as they slowly brought their laughter under control. Léo took a seat in one of the armchairs and leveled a steady gaze at them, while Malik chose to stand on the other side of the coffee table, arms crossed, waiting to find out *what the hell was going on.*

Eventually the pair of them settled enough to actually notice that Malik and Léo were there.

"Oh, hey." Ben sat up and beamed at his lover. "Finished your call?"

Léo pointedly glanced at his watch. "About an hour ago."

"Why didn't you come find me? Hey, Malik, when did you get here?"

Léo sighed and shook his head, but Malik laughed and went to sit in one of the other chairs.

"What were you two talking about?" he asked with open, bald-faced curiosity.

Dani groaned.

"Dani's going to get a job and stay here in Europe for a while," Ben explained. "But she doesn't love me enough to stay in Monaco."

"Ben." Dani sighed. "Be reasonable. Monaco isn't that big. Even if there's a job going that fits my skill set, *and* I manage to get it, it won't pay enough for me to live here. I'd still have to live in France."

"You are always welcome to stay with us, Dani," Léo said politely, and she smiled at him.

"That's sweet, Léo, but not fair to any of us long-term. The truth that Ben just doesn't want to accept is that it's far more practical for me to look for a job and an apartment in Paris or London—or even Nice. I'd still be so much closer than if I was in Australia, and I wouldn't have to be a leech or deal with the sky-high prices here."

Ben pouted. "But you still wouldn't be *here*," he protested. "Sure, we'd be able to catch up more often, but it wouldn't be every day, and realistically, it wouldn't even be every week. It's more likely to end up being once a monthish."

"Which is still a lot more than if I went home," Dani pointed out in a tone that made Malik think it wasn't the first time—or the fifth. "Plus we'll be in the same time zone, or so close that it won't matter. We'll be able to call or text all the time without having to calculate the time difference."

She was being logical and rational, Malik recognized, but he could tell by the look on Ben's face that it didn't matter— and he understood. A tiny part of him, the part he'd pushed deep down and ignored for the past month, the part that still thought maybe he and Dani could have something, was urging him to support Ben's arguments and find a way to keep Dani close at hand.

"You don't know anyone in England," Ben insisted stubbornly, "and you only really know Si and Lucien in Paris."

"So I'll make new friends." This time, Dani sounded less certain.

"And we know people in London and Paris," Léo interjected, the voice of reason. "There's time to introduce her to people. She still needs to arrange for a work visa before any of this can be put into place."

Ben and Dani simultaneously shook their heads.

"I'm an EU citizen," she said. "Well, technically a Croatian citizen, but that means EU now. Oh—I guess London's not really an easy option anymore. I forgot about Brexit."

Malik blinked. "What?" Léo looked just as surprised—it was clearly news to him also.

She looked at him and shrugged. "My dad was born in Croatia and migrated to Australia when he was a child. When my sibs and I were teenagers and Croatia applied to enter the EU, he decided it would be smart to get us citizenship. Since he's a Croatian citizen by birth, we were entitled to apply. So we did."

"Okay," Léo said. "So there's nothing stopping you from getting a job this afternoon and living in Europe for the rest of your life."

"You can work for me," Malik blurted.

Three pairs of eyes turned to him.

"What?" Dani and Ben asked in unison. Léo stared at him as though he'd lost his mind. Maybe he had.

Oh hell. What did I just do?

"Work for you doing what?" Ben demanded, sounding bewildered. "What…. Do you *work*?"

Malik looked to Léo for help but got only a rueful shake of the head. Now that Ben knew Malik worked, he wouldn't rest until he knew details.

"An assistant," he admitted. He'd let the cat out of the bag, and now there was no help for it but to share his biggest secret.

Oh my God.

He leaned back in the chair, suddenly unable to sit up straight.

"Are you all right?" Dani asked in concern. "You've gone dead pale."

Léo got up and went to the drinks cart to pour a hefty slug of brandy into a glass. He brought it to Malik. "Drink this, you idiot. And while your mouth is full, maybe think about what you want to say next."

Malik ignored everything he'd ever been taught about drinking brandy and tossed back the contents of the glass, only feeling a tiny pang of regret for having treated such an excellent brandy so poorly.

"Wow," Ben said. "Someone needs to teach me how to do that. I can manage shots, but if I tried with that much, I'd probably spit it at someone. Or spend twenty minutes coughing and spluttering."

Malik sucked in a breath and laughed, because how could he not?

"Are you okay?" Dani asked, and he met her gaze and let his laugh die down to a smile.

"Yes. Apologies. I suppose I surprised myself."

"You don't need to tell us anything else," Ben said, surprising them all—especially Léo, who fumbled with the drink he was pouring and nearly dropped the glass.

For a moment, Malik considered taking him up on that. He could go back to pretending he was purely the idle rich. Maybe he'd hire an assistant, but it would be one who didn't know his friends and only knew him on a strictly professional basis. His life would continue in the same way, and he'd just go on keeping a huge part of himself secret from most of his closest friends.

"That's okay," he found himself saying. "I think it's time I told more people than just Léo. I'm an author." The words felt strange on his tongue, and he realized he'd never actually said them before. When he'd first told Léo, it had been, "I'm writing a book," and then "I finished the book." Similar for his agent when he'd first submitted a query, and his lawyer and accountant when they'd begun sorting out legal and financial details. Never had he actually said to anyone that he was an author.

Regret burned through him. He was *proud* of his achievements, of his writing career, and yet he'd never shared them with the world. He still didn't want to go public with his identity, but it was definitely time to tell a few select people —Lucien and Simon, his aunt and uncle…, his mother and siblings. And if he had to deal with fallout from his father, well, what else was new?

"That's so cool!" Ben declared.

"What do you write?" Dani asked, leaning forward.

"Suspense thrillers," he told her, and she grinned and whipped out her phone.

"That's my genre," she said, tapping at the screen. "Can I get your books on Amazon? You don't write under your own name, do you? Because I feel like that's something that would have come up on your Wikipedia page."

"Yes, they're on Amazon," he told her. "I write as Raphael Martin."

She froze, and Ben gasped.

"Shut *up*," she whispered. "You're joking. I've *read* your books! I love them—I preorder every one."

Something warm unfurled inside Malik. This was something else he'd been deprived of—the opportunity to interact with fans without the protective, distancing barrier of the internet.

"Thank you," he said solemnly.

"I need signed paperbacks," she demanded. "I'm going to order them right now, and you can sign them to me when they arrive. I always wanted to get signed copies, but the only stores that do them are in Europe and the US, and the shipping was ridiculous—more than the cost of the book."

"You don't need to order them," he told her. "I have copies at home—I'll bring them for you."

Dani looked unsure. "You don't need to do that," she protested, but he waved it away. He quite liked the idea of having more people than just Léo to give his author copies to.

"Ohmigod," Ben said suddenly from where he'd perched on Léo's lap. "Dani, Malik needs *an assistant*."

Oh. Yes. He'd said that.

And he *did* need an assistant.

He turned back to Dani. "It wouldn't be as intense as your previous position," he warned. He'd heard enough from Ben about Dani's job to know that she'd been responsible for the management of a medium-sized office of nearly two hundred people.

"What exactly would the job entail?" she asked. "I may not be the right fit for it—I've never worked in the book industry."

Malik explained briefly about his current social media setup, finishing with, "I'm sure they'd be happy to arrange a handover period, so you'd have time to find your feet. I also want someone to take over organizing the virtual signings— if you wanted, you could expand those, look at arranging some with bookstores in more countries. Manage my email. Maybe do some research, or at least fact-checking. Give me some feedback while I'm writing, and beta read for me. That sort of thing. I'm sure there will be more, but I've never had an assistant before, so I haven't really thought this through."

"That sounds perfect for you, Dan," Ben said. "A change of

pace from your last job, but pretty much complete autonomy. You're awesome at social media stuff, too. And you could stay here in Monaco."

Dani looked torn. "It does sound good," she conceded. "I've gotta say, I'm really interested. But it doesn't change the fact that I would still have to find somewhere over the border to live."

"You could live with me," Malik suggested, and instantly wanted to kick himself. It had to be the brandy this time, because there was no other reason he would say something so *completely asinine*.

"What?"

"*What?*"

"What a great idea!" Ben pronounced gleefully, and Dani stood, walked around the coffee table to stand beside him, and smacked him across the back of the head.

"Excuse him," she said sweetly to Malik. "He's suffering from intense moron-itis."

"Hey!" Ben rubbed his head and glared at her. "Why am I a moron? It *is* a great idea."

Dani lifted her hand again, and Ben curled against Léo for protection.

"It *is*," he insisted, his voice muffled against Léo's neck. "Think about it—Malik has three bedrooms in his apartment, plus the room with the door that's always closed, which I'm now guessing is your office?" He lifted his head and shot an inquiring glance at Malik, who just nodded. He was almost afraid to open his mouth to speak; who knew what might come out next? "Right, so there's plenty of room. You probably don't work set hours, so working out a flexible schedule for your assistant would be more convenient—if you need research or something at eight at night, Dani can put in the time because she'll be *right there*, and then start work later or finish earlier the next day or something. The room can be part of her salary package."

"Perhaps Dani does not want to live and work in the same place," Malik ventured, although it sounded pretty convenient for him. It would also mean he needed to kill any last, lingering thought of taking their personal relationship to a romantic level, because seducing the live-in help was reprehensible, the kind of thing that happened in bad gothic novels and porn movies. "Dani, the offer is open. If you like, we can discuss responsibilities and salary, both with and without a live-in component."

Dani nodded slowly. "I'd like to do some research," she said. "Find out what other author assistant jobs entail, maybe talk to the person handling your social media now, if you can arrange that. It sounds great, and definitely within my range of abilities, but I want to make certain first. It won't do either of us any good if I take the job and it turns out to be a wrong fit."

It was probably wrong that her sensible side turned him on so much, Malik decided. "That's not a problem," he assured her. "I'll get in touch with my agent and have her call you. Take your time thinking about it—as I said, I've never had an assistant before, and although I need one now, I'm not rushing to fill the job."

She smiled. "Okay. That sounds good."

He smiled too. "Good."

They sat there in awkward silence until Ben burst into chatter.

What have I done?

CHAPTER EIGHT

What am I doing?

Dani wondered for the millionth time if she'd been possessed by a mischievous spirit of some kind. What else would have caused her to accept a job and a place to live from the man she was desperately crushing on?

The whole situation just reeked of impending disaster.

Sighing, she sank down on the edge of her bed in Ben and Léo's apartment. At her side, her open suitcase mocked her. She was supposed to be packing for her move to Malik's place, was actually half done, but negative thoughts were delaying her.

Workplace relationships were possible. She knew they were, had been witness to several successful ones. They could also be disastrous. She'd been witness to several of *those* too. Like many things in life, it came down to a case-by-case situation. *But,* a live-in workplace relationship? That ramped up the pressure from the get-go. And add to that a preexisting friendship group....

There were so many ways for things to go wrong—or just be plain icky—that Dani really thought it would be best to completely let go of any notion of a romantic, sexual, or otherwise more than friends and colleagues relationship with Malik.

So. Her heart might be slightly bruised, and her girly bits might be crying out from neglect, but she was still going to take the path that promised a sensible long-term result. Besides, sleeping with the guy who literally paid your salary was a bit creepy. Especially when you also lived in his house.

What the fuck *am I doing?*

Shaking off the little voice that suggested she buy a ticket back to Australia, she got up and finished her packing. It was too late to change her mind now—her cousin was already ensconced in her house, several boxes of her things currently in transit to Monaco—and anyway, why would she want to? This was literally a once-in-a-lifetime opportunity. She had a cushy job working for one of her favorite authors, living in the kind of apartment she would never be able to afford, in Monaco, of all places, with her bestie just a few minutes away and tons of opportunity to explore Europe laid out before her. What was the downside? That she had to get over a crush? She'd done that before, and it wouldn't kill her to do it again.

Big girl undies, Dan.

She'd just zipped her bag when someone knocked on the doorjamb, and she turned her head to see Malik there, smiling at her.

It would be so much easier to get over this crush if he was less... him.

Some men really did have it all. Good looks, charisma, wealth, sense of humor, a winning personality... surely the man had some flaws?

"Are you ready?" he asked, and she nodded.

"Yep!" The cheerful note sounded a little forced, so she tried to cover it by adding, "Thanks for coming to pick me up, but you didn't have to." She could have quite easily walked the distance between his building and Léo's, even if her suitcase hadn't had wheels. It constantly surprised her how small Monaco really was.

"It's no trouble," he assured her, "and it gives me the opportunity to show you how to access the garage. I've added you to the insurance policy in case you need to drive one of the cars."

The breath stalled in Dani's chest, and she had to force her question out on a wheeze. "Do you... uh, have a little runabout I can use?" They hadn't actually discussed her having access to his cars, but it was a nice thought and would certainly be convenient if she needed to go further afield. The thing was, so far the only cars she'd seen him drive had all been waaaaaaaay out of her comfort zone—high-end, high-performance sports cars, the kind she was excited to be a passenger in, but kind of nervous to drive, even if she was insured.

"A... runabout?" Malik sounded uncertain as he stepped into the room and lifted her suitcase off the bed.

"I can take that; it has wheels," she protested, but he shot her a look that had her rolling her eyes and conceding. She would never understand the obsession men had with carrying a woman's luggage, but hey, if he really wanted to do it, it was no skin off her nose. Instead, she scooped up her phone and sunglasses and gave the room a quick once-over for anything she may have forgotten before following him into the hallway.

"Yeah, a runabout," she said, picking up their previous conversation. "Like, a small, inexpensive car that can be used for errands."

Malik laughed.

Stopped in the middle of the hall and flat-out laughed.

"I guess that's a no," she murmured as Ben came to see what was going on.

"Funny joke?" he asked, gaze on Malik, who was still chuckling.

"He offered to let me use his cars and I asked if he had a runabout," Dani explained. To Ben's credit, he managed to restrict himself to a single snort of laughter before he turned to Malik and said, "You've got bigger balls than me."

Dani smacked his arm, indignation stabbing in her chest. She was a good driver, damn him! Definitely better than he was—Ben tended to get distracted behind the wheel.

"I didn't mean it like that," her bestie protested, something that he'd been doing a lot of lately, she realized. "I meant that if my car—*cars*—cost what Malik's do, there's no way I'd let anyone else drive them."

With a sinking feeling, Dani remembered several conversations with Ben about Malik's cars—she'd googled them and knew exactly what they'd cost, and that was before the upgrades Malik had ordered.

There was no way she could drive a car that cost as much as the mortgage on her home.

Rather than start a discussion on that now, she pasted a pleasant smile on her face and said, "We can sort it all out another time. I probably won't need to use a car, anyway—everything's so close here."

Ben's knowing smirk told her he wasn't fooled, but he obligingly led the way to the front door, and then caught her up in a tight hug.

"Oooof! Loosen your grip, Benji," she gasped, and he huffed and let her go.

"Don't call me Benji," he said, pouting, and she planted a kiss on his cheek.

"Relax. I'm not going far, yeah? And I'll call you later." She understood his insecurity. For so many years, they'd been inseparable—at one stage they'd even been roommates. Then he'd moved to Europe and they'd had to get used to a new routine in their relationship. The past six weeks had felt normal, right, and even so minor a change as her moving a few blocks away threatened that.

She was pretty sure there were people who would call that codependent. Lucky for her, she didn't care what they thought.

Taking a deep breath, she followed Malik out of the apartment and into the next phase of her life.

LOOKING at the sheer amount of space left in the walk-in robe-slash-dressing room after she finished unpacking, Dani decided that she really had no choice but to fill it all. All. Every last centimeter. Preferably with things that were wildly impractical. She could keep a drawer or two and maybe a couple feet of hanging space for the practical, everyday things, and then the rest would be a tribute to all the clothes and shoes and accessories that she would rarely wear because they were too unique or impractical or uncomfortable.

Sighing, she reined in her imagination and conceded that the space would stay empty. It might be the kind of room that called out for the wildly unnecessary, but aside from the occasional whimsical splurge, she wasn't that kind of woman. Besides, the dresses she'd bought since arriving were a nod in that direction.

Stepping back into the amazing bedroom, she decided she might as well get to work. Malik had made a point of saying that she should take time to settle in, but now that she was unpacked, the only things she really wanted to do were to explore the apartment or explore her new job, and she'd feel weird snooping through his home while he was there. He'd surely go out and leave her there alone sooner or later, and there would be plenty of time to poke around then. The "basic tour" he'd given her was enough for now.

When she and Malik had been negotiating her duties and salary, he'd asked her if she preferred to have a desk set up in his office or elsewhere. "I can convert the third bedroom to an office for you," he'd offered, and while she'd considered it, ultimately she'd refused. They'd decided to have a small desk for her use added to his office, but she'd requested that he buy her a laptop rather than a desktop computer so she could be mobile. He'd been a little vague on his work patterns when she'd asked, and if it turned out that he needed complete quiet and no distractions, she could easily work from the dining room or the terrace, while still having a dedicated work space in the office.

That was where she went now. Several days earlier, she and Malik had gone shopping for her laptop. He'd been keen to get her something top of the range, while she'd already done research and knew that kind of computing power was unnecessary for her job. In the end they'd compromised, finding something that they were both happy with. Dani smirked as she remembered the dazed expression on the salesman's face by the time they were done arguing over it.

Malik had left a piece of notepaper with the Wi-Fi password and all the account log-ins and passwords that she was likely to need sitting on top of the laptop box. She laid it carefully on the desk, and then tore into the box. The benefit of modern computers and internet was that it really didn't take that long to get things set up, and in less than an hour, she'd installed all the apps she'd need and logged in to all the accounts to get the lay of the land.

She would definitely need to spend some time organizing his cloud backup—it looked like he mostly just saved files randomly, with no folders or filing system at all. How did he find anything? More importantly, how the heck was she supposed to find anything? Everything else was pretty much in order. She'd had a good chat with Aimee, the assistant who'd been managing his social media, so she knew what had been done and what Aimee would have liked to do if she'd had the time. Dani had also made contact with several author assistants online and spoken with them about the general duties they performed. There would still be a learning curve, of course, but she was confident that she could manage without causing any catastrophes. And this job would definitely be lower pressure than her last one.

She was signing up for some online classes in using graphic design software, which she would need to create promotional graphics, when Malik wandered into the room.

"Oh." He stopped short. "I thought you were in your room."

"Nope," Dani said cheerfully. "But I can go if you want—"

"No, no. I was just going to grab some research." He picked up a manila file of printed notes from his desk. "I hope I haven't said anything that made you feel like you had to work right away," he said, frowning.

"Not at all," she assured him, logging in to his email account. "I'm just excited about the job and couldn't wait to get stuck in."

He regarded her silently for a moment, a crease between his brows. "Okay," he said finally. "If you need anything, just ask."

Dani grinned and agreed, and when he left, she sagged in her chair. For fuck's sake, who knew a frown could be sexy?

CHAPTER NINE

The closer it got to the day Malik needed to leave for his sister's wedding, the tenser he got, and it broke Dani's heart. Weddings should be joyous occasions, or at least not unhappy ones. Worse, she didn't want Malik to think that she and Ben had been gossiping about him, so she couldn't say or do anything to make him think that she knew it wasn't going to be a happy trip. So she mostly avoided talking about it unless it couldn't be avoided—like when she made his travel arrangements—and then she kept it strictly to the matter at hand, not letting herself ask questions like she would have with anyone else.

For the most part, working for Malik was a dream. She'd gotten over the initial hurdle of logging in to all his accounts, reorganizing his files, and establishing contact with his agent, editor, and lawyer within the first few days, and had spent hours going through his books to pull out lines that could be used for teasers. She'd combed through the social media profiles of authors within his genre, noting what got great responses and from whom, and she'd introduced herself as his assistant on his accounts. She and Malik had decided from the beginning that it would be best for her to post as herself, rather than trying to pass off her voice as his. He'd promised to sit down with her once a week to compile a few posts in his own voice for her to schedule on his behalf. Dani had scheduled the time in both their calendars, beginning last week and stretching on into perpetuity. Already, activity on his accounts had picked up, and she was planning some interactive contests and giveaways that would hopefully bump things a bit more.

Malik himself had sighed with relief when she took over his email inbox, and then again as she began taking on the administrative duties he hated. Anytime she suggested something or asked for something, he agreed immediately, and he'd gladly handed over his credit card details so she could set up advertising accounts. "Whatever you think best," he'd told her. "Just keep track of it all." So she'd created a spreadsheet that she could input everything into until she had time to research appropriate bookkeeping software.

The only downside, apart from Malik's current gloomy mood, was that every time she looked up from her laptop, he was there. Handsome, focused, a little crease between his brows as he typed industriously, writing his latest sure-to-be brilliant book. Or if she was working elsewhere in the apartment, he'd come and politely offer her a coffee, or tease that she was working too hard and coax her away from her computer for a break. He was a terrible-yet-endearing cook, a tidy and considerate roommate, intelligent, funny, and driving her utterly mad with want.

Unfortunately for her, it seemed that having her work for him had flipped a switch in his brain. She no longer felt any kind of interested vibe from him. He was friendly in a way that crossed most employer-employee boundaries, but that was to be expected given their previous friendship and connections. But he never indicated by word, deed, or look that he wanted more.

And even though Dani had made the decision not to pursue her feelings, knowing that he no longer wanted her sucked. Which made her feel stupid, because she was an adult woman, not a sappy teenager who thought angst à la *Romeo and Juliet* was romantic and exciting. Far better that they both moved past the attraction and got on with their lives than that they moped in forbidden longing.

Right?

Ben was utterly frustrated that his grand plan was not working out, though, and that gave Dani a certain amount of satisfaction.

She finished replying to fan mail and switched over to check social media. Earlier she'd scheduled the next few days' posts, but she wanted to get on top of the notifications.

It didn't take long to go through and like or love people's posts and comments, leaving comments where necessary, and she was nearly done when she got to one that made her laugh out loud.

"Malik!" she called. He was in the kitchen, making coffee. "You've gotta see this!"

She heard him moving around, and a moment later he came into the room. "What is it?"

Grinning, she waved a hand at the laptop screen. "Come and see."

With a faintly curious expression, he crossed the room and came to stand behind her, bending to see the screen… and laughed.

"That's fantastic! Who is that?" Delight rang in his voice.

"Duh, one of your fans. I'll bet you never expected to see one of your characters cosplayed." She clicked on the image, enlarging it, and marveled at the level of detail in the costume.

"Never," he agreed. "But now that I have, I want to see it all the time. Can we print that picture? Have you responded to him yet?"

"Not yet. Do you want to do it?" She turned her head to look at him just as he leaned in and reached for the keyboard and ended up with her face far too close to the smooth skin of his neck. Inhaling, she breathed in his scent—some ridiculously expensive cologne that was worth every cent, plus whatever it was about him that appealed to her on a base level. Pheromones, maybe? God, just the smell of him was enough to make her girly bits sit up and take notice.

He drew back, and their gazes met. Held.

Heat flushed up from her chest.

Her lips parted on a pant.

She should look away.

She should move back.

She should have never taken this job, because if she hadn't, she'd be free to lunge forward and climb him like a monkey would a tree.

That thought was what broke the spell, and she rolled her chair far enough away to stand without touching him. "Here, you should sit while you reply. I'll… uh, go finish up the coffee."

"Dani—"

She didn't hear whatever he'd been about to say, already out the door and moving down the hallway. By the time she got to the kitchen, she felt more in control.

For about five seconds.

Because Malik followed her.

"Dani, this is ridiculous."

Er… what?

"What's ridiculous?" she asked as innocently as she could manage, really hoping that he didn't know about her crush.

Pffft. Crush. The truth was, she was more than halfway in love with him.

"This. The two of us pretending that we're not… pretending that we're friends."

Ouch.

"We're not friends?" She wasn't able to keep the hurt from her voice.

"Of course we're friends," he replied impatiently. "You're one of my best friends. But that's not all we are."

Warmed by the knowledge that he valued her friendship as much as she did his, she was tempted to gloss over his last comment… but Malik wasn't stupid, and this tension between them wasn't going away.

"We're friends," she insisted. "And you're my boss. That's all."

Sighing, he leaned his hips against the kitchen counter, and she tried not to let her gaze drop. That position put his entire groin area into prominence.

"I don't want to be the creepy employer who hits on his assistant," he began, "but this thing between us is getting out of control. I can barely concentrate on what I'm doing when you're in the room."

Dani jerked. "I… I can work in here," she declared. "I'm so sorry, I didn't reali—"

"Stop, Dani. That's not what I mean. That won't fix things. I've been thinking about this a lot. Originally I decided things had to be platonic between us because you work for me *and* live with me, and I would be the worst person in the world to start something up with you in those circumstances. But you're not subordinate to me at all—"

"I bloody well think not!"

He grinned. "If we were together, you wouldn't let the fact that I pay you impact our relationship. You wouldn't let the fact that I pay you pressure you into a relationship with me. Right?"

"Right. But all that presupposes that I want to be in a relationship with you. I don't," she lied.

His dark eyes studied her, and then he smiled. It was a charming, mischievous smile, and it filled Dani with dread.

"So you don't feel any attraction to me? No sexual tension?"

Unable to lie in the face of the evidence, because it was pretty obvious, Dani said, "Of course I do. But it's just... curiosity."

What.

What the hell had she just said?

"Curiosity?" Malik raised a brow in a supercilious way that made her want to slap him.

"Yes." She forged on. "You're hot. There's a spark between us. And because you're off-limits, my imagination has blown the spark out of proportion. It would never come to anything. Surface attraction."

"Surface attraction," he repeated, and she nodded vehemently.

"Yes. We both feel it because we know nothing can ever happen between us. Like when you're on a diet and you really want a triple-fudge cupcake with a huge swirl of icing. Normally, you would never eat it because it's too rich, but once you can't have it, that's all you want." Dismally, Dani wondered if she was setting herself up to fail, because she'd never met a triple-fudge cupcake she hadn't eaten. And licked the paper it came in.

The wicked gleam in Malik's eyes told her she'd said the wrong thing.

"Well, this should be easy to resolve, then," he declared, and butterflies took flight in her stomach.

"Oh?" she croaked as he straightened.

"Yes. It's simple. If this is just surface attraction, if we really *don't* want each other but are being drawn together by some form of reverse psychology our own brains are imposing… then we should kiss."

What?

"What?" Kiss him? Oh no. That would be bad. Very, very bad.

But oh, so good.

"Kiss me. If you really don't want me, you'll know immediately. This tension between us will go away. But if not…."

His words hung in the air.

Dani hesitated.

He sauntered closer, until he was standing in her space, barely a breath away, surrounding her with his scent and heat. "Come on, Dani. Bite the cupcake," he whispered.

Bite the…?

She laughed.

And he swooped, taking her mouth in a kiss that made her forget about cupcakes and friendship and any reason she might have had for not wanting this.

Not want this? Was she crazy?

By the time they came up for air, there was no pretending she didn't want him. Her arms were around his neck, hands dug into his gorgeous soft hair, body draped full-length against his. He smiled down at her, lips slightly puffy, eyes heavy-lidded.

"Surface attraction?" he murmured, and she roused herself from her kiss-induced stupor and pinched the back of his neck. "Ow!"

"You deserved that," she said, pulling away and running a hand through her hair. She was hot and flushed and couldn't say she was sorry. "This is not good."

"I think that hurt more than the pinch," he muttered. "Not good?"

"Not the kiss." She waved that idea away. Nobody in the known universe could say that kiss wasn't good. "The situation. It's so messy, Malik."

Sighing, he took her shoulders in his hands and stroked his thumbs over her bare collarbone. She shivered, unable to help the response.

"It's messy," he agreed. "But it's also not. We're both strong people, correct? Neither of us is likely to let the other bulldoze us?"

She thought about that for a moment. Malik was her boss, true, but she'd never let a boss bully her before. She'd certainly never let a boyfriend bully her. It was unlikely she'd let anything like that happen now. And she wasn't the type to use her personal influence with her boss to change things at work—or to use what happened at work as leverage against her boyfriend. Plus, it wasn't like she could use sex with the boss as a way to get ahead in the office. She *was* the office. There was no career progression in this job unless she left it and went to work elsewhere.

"Correct," she conceded finally.

"Do you have doubts about whether we'd be good together?"

It was a serious question, but she could tell he already knew the answer.

"No." She'd long ago had to admit that Ben was right—she and Malik would be perfect for each other.

"So as long as we respect each other at work, what's stopping us?"

She lifted her hands and cupped his cheeks, feeling the faint bristle of his five o'clock shadow. "I'm afraid," she said bluntly. "I... feel so much for you. It's easier if we're just friends and colleagues, because if it's more, I could fall in love with you so easily. And if you broke my heart, it would hurt worse than anything ever before." The brutal honesty left her bared and vulnerable in a way she did not like, but she needed Malik to know how serious this was for her. And she knew, deep down to her soul, that he would never use her honesty to hurt her. If he didn't see this becoming a serious, long-term relationship, better that they both knew that now.

He swallowed hard.

"Dani, if things go bad between us, it could potentially damage my relationship with Léo. Definitely with Ben. If someone had told me three months ago that I would risk that, I would have laughed at them as I booted them out the door. You are the only person, ever, that I would consider taking that risk for." His gaze on her was steady, and having seen the connection between him and Léo, she understood what he was saying.

He was in this.

She nodded.

The smile that broke out on his face was so beautiful, it made her heart ache. A matching grin stretched her mouth, and then she shrieked as he bent and lifted her in a fireman carry.

"Malik! What are you doing?"

He put her down. "I thought that was obvious."

Suddenly, she felt shy. "I'm… at work," she stammered, and then wanted to kick herself for being such an idiot.

He seemed to get it, though, and his wicked grin flashed again. "It's break time," he declared. "Want to make out in the break room?"

She shouted with laughter as he closed in, and gladly went into his arms.

By the time they'd cleaned up their dinner dishes, Dani had been kissed in the "break room," in the office, in the living room, and in the hallway. She'd kissed Malik on the terrace while he was grilling steaks, and he'd liked that so much that he'd nearly burned their dinner. Her mouth was swollen and tender, but she didn't care. Kissing Malik was her new favorite thing to do.

"Want to watch a movie?" he asked, and something in his tone told her they wouldn't see much of the movie. That was okay with her.

"Sure. You pick; I'm going to change into my pajamas." She wandered off toward her bedroom with seeming casualness, but as soon as she was out of earshot, she ran.

In her room, she went directly to the drawer that held her underwear. When she'd gone shopping with Ben, right after arriving in Monaco, she'd fallen in love with an entirely impractical and absurdly overpriced silk nightgown. It was completely unsuitable for sleeping in—it really only had one purpose, and that was to be taken off. Ben had nearly choked when he'd seen the price tag, and it had made her hesitate for a long time, but in the end she'd been unable to resist the whisper-soft hand-painted silk, reasoning that it was a once-in-a-lifetime splurge. Now, she was glad she'd given in to temptation, donning the cerulean nightgown with the satisfaction of knowing she wouldn't be wearing it for long.

"Dani! I'm starting the movie!" Malik shouted. Dani smiled smugly. Not that long ago, he never would have shouted across the apartment, instead coming to find her. She credited herself for loosening him up, at least when he was with her.

"I'm coming!" she called back, checking her reflection one last time before turning off the light and leaving the room.

The movie that was playing when she returned to the living room was an action flick she vaguely recognized—one with a loose plot and a lot of macho explosions. The kind of movie it was easy to zone out if you planned to not watch much of it. Grinning, she strolled over to the back of the couch and rolled over it directly onto Malik, who was stretched out along the length.

He yelped.

"What are—" His eyes went wide as he actually looked at her, hands automatically lifting to hold her waist. "Oh."

"Oh?" She arched a brow.

He swallowed, his gaze tracking down her body.

"Oh," he croaked.

"How much did you want to watch this movie?"

He breathed deeply. "Right now? Not at all."

"Good answer." She leaned down and captured his mouth with hers. This kiss went from zero to a hundred in milliseconds, hot and wet. Malik's hands on her waist burned through the barely there silk of the nightgown, but it really wasn't enough—she wanted them on her body.

She pulled back from the kiss, ignoring Malik's murmur of protest, and sat up, being careful not to maim him.

"Dani," he began, his dark, slumberous gaze locked on her.

"Shh." She grasped the hem of the nightie and slowly drew it up, keeping her eyes on his for as long as she could before pulling it over her head. Finally naked, she tossed the silky garment aside—although the part of her that remembered how much it cost made her check to make sure it hadn't landed on the floor.

It hadn't.

When she looked back at Malik, he was staring at her in a way that made her feel completely powerful.

"Your turn," she suggested, and the words seemed to bring him back to himself.

That wicked smirk tilted his lips.

"Why don't you do it?" he asked, leaning back against the couch arm in a way that made her think of an emperor reclining on his throne.

She arched a brow. "You say that like you think it's a challenge." Leaning forward, she undid a few shirt buttons, then slid her hand inside. His skin was warm, lightly furred, and just the act of having her hand on him ramped up the tension between them.

He sat up, catching her unaware, and kissed her, his hands going back to her waist and then moving up her back in a smooth slide that made her shiver. Her nipples, already erect, went so hard it almost hurt—from having him touch *her back*. If she'd needed proof that she wanted him, she had it.

In the next moment, he was cupping her breasts, his thumbs teasing her nipples, and she moaned and moved to straddle him, wanting to be closer. The fabric of his pants, ridiculously soft and smooth as it was, irritated her when it came into contact with the inside of her thighs. She wanted him naked, skin to skin.

"You need to be naked," she demanded, breaking their kiss again and attacking his shirt with fervor.

Huffing out a breathless laugh, he helped her get his shirt off, then shifted her off him so he could stand. Hands on the waist of his pants, he paused.

"What are you doing?" she asked indignantly. Was he *stopping*? She squeezed her legs together. No fucking way!

"I don't have anything here," he said. "We should move to my bedroom."

Oh.

"Okay." She scrambled off the couch, and they headed down the hallway, leaving their clothes strewn around and the TV on.

Some things were more important.

Malik's bedroom was fantastic. She'd seen it in passing but had never been inside. It was furnished in warm woods, with plush, jewel-toned fabrics and sumptuous leather. His bedcover was an ocean of quilted blue silk that she wanted to roll around on.

There's a thought....

She strolled nonchalantly past him, making sure to add a bit of a sway to her naked hips, and collapsed gracefully—she hoped—onto the bed, lying back on the deliciously soft, cool silk and moaning her pleasure.

Malik's pants hit the floor and a second later, he was beside her.

"If I could paint, I would paint a portrait of you like this," he said hoarsely, skimming a finger slowly down the center of her chest. "You are amazing." He lowered his head and licked her nipple, keeping his eyes on her face the entire time, and when she smiled, her breath hitching a little, he opened his mouth and sucked it inside. She closed her eyes, luxuriating in the sensation, lifting her hand to tangle it in his hair and hold him to her. This was the best kind of dream come true; his scent, the warmth of him, the weight of him. His touch. Her whole body yearned to be closer.

He lavished attention on the other nipple, and then just when Dani was beginning wonder if she would actually come from that alone, something that had never happened to her before, he began to kiss his way down her torso. Over her stomach, pausing to kiss her navel, the faint rasp of his five o'clock shadow a tease against her sensitive skin.

"Malik, you're killing me," she gasped when he traced his tongue along the crease of her thigh. He came deliciously close to where she so desperately wanted him... then drew away.

Hissing, she grabbed his head, and he laughed and

lowered it, that talented tongue darting out and flicking her clit.

Dani's eyes rolled back in her head as he settled down to work. *Yes!*

Malik's talents lay in more than just words.

The tension in her grew higher and higher, and she had to force herself not to squeeze her thighs around his head, not to clench her fists in his hair, not to….

Stars exploded behind her eyelids, and for a moment she stopped breathing.

As her brain slowly came back online and she lay panting desperately for breath, she became aware of Malik lying beside her. She dragged her eyelids open to see him propped on an elbow, smirking smugly.

"That was acceptable," she wheezed, and he laughed, a delighted sound that both thrilled her and made her want to punch him.

Right.

"Where are the condoms?"

He gestured toward his groin, and she saw that he was already wearing one.

Good.

Surging up, she took him by surprise and knocked him over onto his back, straddling him before he could regain his composure. A moment later, she was lowering herself over his cock.

It had been a while for her, and he wasn't exactly small anyway, so she eased down carefully, taking her time and enjoying the stretch, the rub against each and every nerve ending.

The sound that came from Malik made her feel like a goddess.

By the time she'd taken all of him, there was a sheen of

sweat on his forehead and he was swallowing convulsively, his gaze fixed on her face.

So she tightened all *those* muscles.

"Fuck, Dani…." His hips jerked under her.

"Shh. It's my turn to play." She leaned forward, pulling partly off him, and kissed him, then straightened again, tightening everything as she slid back, and his groan was music to her ears.

Then she took pity on him—and herself, because his dick felt incredible inside her, and she wanted *more*—and began to move.

It didn't take long. Dani went first, despite her best efforts to hold out, and no sooner had she cried out, every muscle clenching, than Malik surged into a sitting position and rolled her over. She barely had time to suck in a breath before he was thrusting, once, twice, hard, in a way that made her think maybe she could—

He yelled, his face pulling into a rictus of pleasure that was so beautiful to her.

And then he collapsed, catching himself on his elbows at the last second, a small courtesy that just confirmed her suspicion that she was already halfway in love with him.

And she was totally okay with that.

CHAPTER TEN

They spent a long time discussing the best way to tell Léo about them. They were certain he'd be happy as long as they were happy, but still, it was a potentially messy situation and he was bound to have concerns.

"We could just let Ben do it," Malik suggested as they lay in bed being lazy Sunday morning a week later, and although Dani made the appropriate shocked and reproving noises, she considered the idea.

Which Malik knew, the bastard. Sometimes it seemed like he knew her better than she knew herself. She'd never been in a relationship that was so instantly comfortable. She could be entirely herself, and they just fit seamlessly into each other's lives. Add the insanely hot sex to that, and there was really nothing more that she wanted.

"No, we can't do that," she finally declared. "He's your best friend, and he'll be hurt if he finds out from anyone else." They weren't worried at all about telling Ben. Her bestie was not subtle about his matchmaking attempts. "We should do it soon. Now. Call and invite them for brunch." She sat up and did a mental inventory of the pantry and fridge.

"Now?" Malik protested, running a hand down her naked back. "I thought we could...."

She leaned over and kissed him. "We will. Call Léo, and then we'll have"—she grabbed his wrist and looked at his watch—"an hour before we have to get up."

"Or I could not call Léo, and we'd have a lot more time." He pressed a kiss to her palm and smiled charmingly.

"Or I could call Ben and tell them to come right now," Dani replied sweetly. "The longer you leave this, the worse it will be. How would you feel if you were in Léo's place and you found out weeks later?"

Malik sighed. "Fine. You're right. Hand me my phone."

Dani grabbed it, and then yelped when it began ringing in her hand. "It's Lucien," she said, passing it to Malik. As he answered, she got out of bed. Even if he wrapped up both conversations quickly, it would take him a few minutes, and she needed to use the bathroom anyway.

When she got back, he was staring glumly at his phone. "What's wrong? Is everything okay with Lucien and Si?"

"Yes." He pulled her close and kissed her deeply, then pulled back and crushed her dreams for morning sex. "They flew down this morning to surprise us all. Brunch has been brought forward to thirty minutes from now. I already called Léo and told him." The mournful tone made her chuckle.

"That sucks," she said frankly, "but I guess we can just spend the afternoon fucking on the balcony."

He brightened. "You would do that? You're the best girlfriend ever!"

Dani shrugged, took his hand, and tugged him out of bed. "It looks straight out over the ocean, and the angle of the railing means nobody on a boat could see anything. So, sure. Now go shower while I check if we need anything, and then you can go to the supermarket while I shower."

"Or we can just call downstairs to the concierge desk and

they'll arrange for everything you need to be delivered," Malik said over his shoulder as he wandered naked toward the en suite bathroom. Dani was distracted by his muscled back and ass, but still shook her head at the reminder of the level of wealth and privilege Malik was used to.

Fortunately, she'd just done a shop a few days before and the kitchen was well-stocked. By the time she heard a key in the front door half an hour later, they were both showered, dressed, and breakfast was half done.

"Hey!" Ben bounced into the kitchen and came over to kiss her cheek. "Thanks for cooking. I love the yacht club, but it's nice to have brunch at home sometimes."

"No problem. Can you get the juice out of the fridge?" Dani focused on staying casual. She'd seen Ben in person three times since she and Malik had hooked up, but never while Malik was there too. She knew Ben suspected something was going on with her, but so far he hadn't pushed. It was, however, extremely likely that he'd see the new dynamic between her and Malik and *guess*. Most people failed to give Ben credit for being observant, but he really was.

Fortunately, Lucien came in then. "Dani, there you are." He swooped in to kiss her cheek. "I hope you don't mind us invading like this. Simon and I couldn't decide how to spend our Sunday, and what better than a day with friends?"

"It's great to see you," Dani said sincerely. "Where's Si?"

"Here." Si dodged around Ben, who was carrying the orange juice out to the dining room, and came to hug her. "What's this about you living here now? Ben was telling me the other week, but I still don't get it."

Shit. Shitshitshit. With all the "how do we tell people" tension over her and Malik hooking up, she'd completely forgotten that Lucien and Simon didn't know Malik was an author. What reason had they been given for her moving in?

"Uh—"

"Actually," Malik broke in smoothly from the doorway, "that's something I wanted to talk to you about. I've been waiting to tell you until I saw you in person." He was looking at Lucien, who raised an eyebrow.

"Sounds serious. Is everything okay?"

"Absolutely," Malik assured. "Just… something I should have told you a long time ago."

The oven buzzed with impeccable timing. "Breakfast's ready," Dani said brightly. "Head on through and I'll bring it out."

"I'll help," Malik said, which neatly saved him from the questions burning in Lucien's gaze.

Five minutes later, the food had been served and they were settled in at the table. Dani forked up some of the frittata and pretended not to notice that Ben was staring a hole into the side of her head.

"Malik, the suspense is killing me," Lucien declared, then turned to Léo. "What's this all about?"

"Why are you asking me?"

Lucien waved a hand dismissively. "Please. As if Malik has ever had a secret from you."

Dani choked.

Fortunately, Si didn't have to pound *too* hard on her back before she was breathing again.

"Sorry," she rasped. "Went down the wrong way."

Malik shook his head, smiling wryly, then said to Lucien, "Wait just a moment."

He got up and left the room, returning quickly—which Dani was thankful for, as Ben had seemingly grown even more suspicious and she was sure she was turning red under his stare.

Malik handed Lucien a paperback book—one of his.

Lucien took it and turned it over, studying it from all angles. "I know this author," he said. "Léo's got all his books.

Are you starting a book club or something?" The question was teasing and entirely rhetorical, but Malik answered anyway.

"Not exactly."

Idly, Lucien opened the book, flipping through the front matter, then stilled. "Oh, it's signed. Did you meet the auth —" He stopped and stared at the title page. "It's signed to me." He looked up. "In your handwriting. Is this a joke?"

Malik shook his head, and Dani held her breath.

"You wrote this?"

"Yes."

"You wrote all those books?"

"Yes." Malik's voice was tight now, and Dani wished she could go to him, hold his hand.

"You...." Lucien looked back down at the book in his hand. "How the hell did you keep this a secret?"

"It wasn't easy." Some of the tension had eased now, and then it disappeared entirely when Lucien broke out in a grin.

"I knew you were up to something, you sneaky bastard. No way could you not be bored out of your mind just living off investments and partying—especially these last few years, with less of the parties. I wish you'd told me."

Dani grinned.

"I wish I had too," Malik said frankly. "Léo was the only one who knew—first it didn't seem real enough to tell anyone, and then... I don't know. I'm glad you know now, though."

"This is so impressive." Si reached over and took the paperback from Lucien. "I've seen these books at Léo's— there are a lot of them. That's brilliant, Malik."

"Six so far," Malik confirmed. "Number seven releases in October, and eight is in edits now."

"Eight books." Lucien shook his head. "You blow my

mind, Malik. I'm so proud of you. I have to read these books now."

"You really do," Léo told him. "I've been nagging you to for years. If you had, you might have guessed before now."

"Really?" Lucien took the book from Si and flipped a few pages, as though thinking about starting right away, but Si stole it back and got up to put it on the sideboard.

"You can read it later. Not around food, though, because it's a signed copy and you don't want to ruin it."

Malik laughed. "If he does, I have more," he began, but Si shook his head.

"Nope. If you want to gift him a copy, that's really nice of you. But if he wrecks it, he has to replace it."

Lucien waggled his eyebrows and said, "Look at you, getting all authoritative," and they all laughed.

"Anyway," Malik went on, "that's why Dani's staying here. She's taken on the herculean job of being my assistant, and it worked out easier all round for it to come with room and board."

"Oh." Si sounded disappointed, and Lucien nudged him.

"Do you want to try that again?"

Somewhat abashed, Si said, "No, sorry—I'm glad you've gotten a job here, Dani, and that you're staying. I just…. When Ben said you'd moved in here…. Uh…. I had—a different impression, that's all." He sounded embarrassed as hell by the time he stammered to a stop, and Dani couldn't blame him. After all, as far as he knew, she and Malik were just employer and employee, and he'd basically just said that he'd thought they were together. Which they were. But he didn't know that.

Fuck, it was confusing. She looked across the table at Malik, who was looking at her, an eyebrow raised.

She nodded.

He turned to Léo. "There's something I need to tell you.

All of you." He swept his gaze around the table to take in the rest of them.

Léo set down his fork. "Something good, or something for which we need to call the lawyer?"

Ben pinched him. "Léo! Malik doesn't need our help to call the lawyer."

"Thank you, Ben," Malik said dryly. "The confidence you have in me is inspiring. No, Léo, you don't need to call the lawyer. It's good. Wonderful, in fact."

"Don't keep us in suspense," Lucien piped in. "Honestly, Malik, all these secrets are giving me heartburn."

"Dani and I are seeing each other," Malik said, and the table fell silent. Léo's mouth dropped open.

"Seeing each other?" he repeated faintly, and Dani couldn't blame him. Could Malik have made it sound any more bland?

"We hooked up," she blurted, and all eyes turned to her.

"You bitch," Ben declared. "*How* could you not tell me? I *knew* you were keeping something secret from me. After everything I've done to get you two together, how could you not have told me the second it happened?" He was working himself up into full melodrama, but Léo interrupted.

"After everything you've done to get them together? What the hell has been going on?" He sounded incredulous. Ben rolled his eyes.

"Honestly, Léo, how did you miss it? I haven't exactly been keeping it secret. Why do you think I was so keen for Dani to move in here?"

Léo shook his head, seemingly still unable to get his head around it, and Dani began to worry. She'd known he'd be surprised, but she'd hoped he'd also be happy.

"Well, I'm thrilled to hear it. Congratulations, both of you. I knew you'd be great together," Si said, and Dani smiled gratefully at him.

"Thank you. It's still pretty new."

"You'll never get away from us now," Lucien warned, his eyes twinkling. "You've been assimilated."

"Like I'd ever have left anyway," she scoffed.

Léo got up and came around the table to kiss her cheek. "I'm sorry if I sounded less than enthusiastic, Dani," he said. "I am happy for you, if you're happy. I was just surprised—but this is wonderful news." He returned to his seat, and Dani beamed in relief. Across the table, Malik was smiling too.

"And that's all the secrets we have," he concluded.

"I think that's enough for today." Dani chuckled. "Unless anyone else has something they want to share?"

Ben pouted. "I'm not talking to you."

"You got your way," she protested. "Why are you so grumpy?"

"Because you're supposed to tell me these things!"

"We may as well eat," Malik said. "This conversation could go on for a while."

Léo snorted, and Ben swung an ireful glare on him. Dani decided she should head this off before it got out of control.

"I'm sorry I didn't tell you sooner, but it's very new and we were still working it out. We both wanted to be together, but it's a complicated situation and we had some reservations. You're the first people to know."

Ben sniffed, but then spoiled it by grinning. "I was right," he crowed. "You two are perfect together, aren't you? Hah!"

And he didn't let it go until they'd finished eating.

CHAPTER ELEVEN

alik sighed in satisfaction as he closed the document and shut down his laptop. His work for the day was officially done—target number of pages edited, word count met. His time was now completely his own, and he knew exactly what he wanted to do with it.

For the five weeks he and Dani had been together, things had been great. Fantastic, even. But a few days ago, he'd realized that he'd cheated her out of the early stages of their relationship. They'd never dated, just gone straight to living together. Didn't she deserve to get dressed up and be taken out to a nice restaurant?

He'd been remiss.

Tonight, he'd fix that.

He'd made reservations at a small but excellent restaurant nearby. Ben had already taken Dani to his favorite restaurants in the area, but somehow they hadn't yet made it to this place, for which Malik was grateful.

This morning over breakfast, he'd asked Dani to go on a date with him. She'd laughed, surprised, but when he'd explained, her dark gaze had gone all soft and gooey, and she'd kissed him until they both were breathless.

Then she'd declared she wanted a new outfit for their "first date" and called Ben, who'd whined about having to go shopping so loudly that Malik had heard him through the phone.

She'd gotten home about an hour ago, laden down with shopping bags and smiling brightly. For that smile alone, Malik wished he'd thought of this earlier. But it was foolish to dwell on the past, especially when he needed to get ready.

It was time to take his amazing girlfriend out on a date.

THIS WAS the best thing he'd done in years. Maybe ever. Dani's face had been so soft and warm and happy all night. She was always beautiful, and she'd gone to a lot of trouble getting ready for the evening, but that wasn't what made him unable to keep his eyes off her. It was the way she looked at him. Nobody had ever looked at him that way.

They hadn't officially been together long, but they'd known each other a long time, counting all their incidental Skype conversations and secondhand interactions through Léo and Ben. He knew her, the person she was, and more importantly, he knew the person she was with him. And she knew him, more than anyone in the world except maybe Léo —but he was certain that would change in time. He didn't need to pretend with her—didn't need to be Malik al-Saud, society dilletante and darling of the tabloids, witty, charming, devil-may-care. He could just be Malik, who wrote books, loved his friends, liked to have fun, and avoided his father at all costs.

As they left the restaurant, he reached out and took her

hand. She smiled at him in the way that made him feel warm inside, and suggested, "Let's walk home."

He raised a brow. He'd arranged for a car and driver for the evening, not wanting to be distracted by driving or finding parking. "Are you sure?"

Dani shrugged. "Yeah. It's not far, and it's a beautiful night."

It *was* a beautiful night, perfect for lovers to stroll, but… "Can you manage in those shoes?" They were deliciously sexy concoctions of straps and stiletto heels, and he wanted to see her wearing only them later, not throwing them off the balcony as she cursed the day they'd been made.

"My feet will be sore," she admitted, "but not crippled. It's really only a few blocks, Malik."

Conceding the point, he sent the driver away and they began their stroll home. It really wasn't far at all, and if her feet got too sore, he could probably carry her. She might even find that romantic.

He laughed out loud. Not his practical Dani.

"What?" she asked, and when he told her, she laughed too. "Sorry, hon, I'd be so busy berating myself that I wouldn't notice if it was romantic or not." She squeezed his hand. "But the thought is lovely. Maybe we can role play it someday— me being the foolish damsel and you sweeping in to rescue me."

Malik stopped dead in the street, took her by the shoulders, and kissed her soundly. "I love you," he said, and they were the easiest words he'd ever said, felt more right than anything else in the world. "I love you because you're clever, kind, beautiful, and the best person I've ever met. But also because you've never been a foolish damsel in your life and if you ever needed rescuing, you'd do it yourself and probably rescue your would-be rescuer right along with you." He pulled a face. "I feel as though I've said 'rescue' too many times. If that were a sentence in one of my books, my editor would make me change it."

Dani laughed, but it was a wet sound, and when she leaned up to kiss him, there were tears on her cheeks. "I love you," she murmured.

Everything in him relaxed. Tension drained away. All was right with the world. Dani loved him.

They stood there in the street, kissing, not caring who saw them, for a long time.

"Let's go home," Dani whispered finally, running her hands over his chest through his shirt. "You can carry me from the front door to the bed."

Malik had never considered himself old-fashioned, but something primitive in him fired at the thought of carrying his woman to their bed. It must have shown on his face, because she chuckled. He grabbed her hand and tugged her along.

"Let's go faster."

"I don't want to." Even to his own ears, he sounded like a petulant child.

Dani sighed. She'd been incredibly patient, but he could tell it was starting to wear thin.

"Malik, not packing doesn't mean you don't have to go. It just means you won't have clean underwear, a toothbrush, or anything appropriate to wear to the wedding when you get there."

He bit back a smile, not done yet with his sulk. He was due to leave early the next morning. The wedding wasn't for several days yet, but Aunt Miryam had insisted he travel with them, and he really hadn't been able to think of a reason not to that wouldn't offend his entire family. Besides, he did want to see Houria and spend a little time with her before she got married. He was staying a few days after the wedding, also, but she wouldn't be around then. It would be good to see his mother and sisters and his oldest brother, who was a good man. His other brother, not so much.

"Come on," Dani coaxed. "The sooner you pack, the sooner it will be done and we can do other things." Her look was very direct, and parts of Malik stood to attention.

"Fine." He heaved himself out of his chair. "But those other things had better be good."

"Are you saying there are times when they're not good?" She followed him out of the office and down the hall to their bedroom.

"No," Malik said immediately, because he was no fool. Anyway, it was true. "I just mean there had better be extra goodness."

Dani sat in the armchair in the dressing room and watched him get out his overnight bag and garment bag. "I think some extra goodness can be arranged. We're both going to need it to tide us over until you get back."

For the hundredth time in the past month, he wondered if he should bring her with him, and for the hundredth time, he reminded himself why it was a bad idea.

"Stop that," she said softly. "We've talked about this. Our relationship is still pretty new, and there's enough strain between you and your father without springing me on him at a big family event. Your mother will be busy with the wedding and doesn't need the distraction of meeting her son's girlfriend. And the whole situation is made more complicated because I'm Ben's friend. There will be plenty of opportunities for me to meet your family. Now is not the right time."

She knew him so well. He sighed and dumped some underwear into his bag. "I just don't want to be away from you."

"It's only a week," she consoled, "and we both have phones. We can talk every day."

"Text me," he demanded, and she raised an eyebrow.

"Bossy much?"

"Text me, please." Even to him, it didn't sound less like an order, and she snorted.

"I can text you. I probably would have anyway. Is there anything in particular you want me to say?" The mock sweetness of her tone warned him that he'd better answer that carefully.

"Whatever you want. You always know what to say." He ducked as she threw a balled-up pair of socks at him. Where had they even come from? He kept his socks across the room from the armchair.

"It's going to be fine, Malik," she said, getting up and coming over to kiss him briefly. "You'll have fun. It's a party, after all. Just don't let your dad get to you, and you'll be back here before you know it."

She wandered out into the bedroom, and Malik wished he had her confidence.

❧

FIVE DAYS LATER, Dani was struggling to hold back an appreciative moan when the trill of a phone sounded from the other room. She ignored it and took another bite of the luscious steak Léo had grilled. Dinner with her bestie and his boyfriend had been an inspired idea. The apartment had felt so lonely since Malik left—she had tons of work to keep her busy, Malik called every day, and they texted frequently, but she still missed him like crazy.

The phone stopped, then immediately began again. Neither Ben nor Léo reacted—they'd long since designated dinner a phone-free time—and she could tell from the ring-tone that it wasn't hers, so she wasn't worried.

Until it started ringing for a third time.

That couldn't be good.

She exchanged glances with Ben, who put down his glass and said to Léo, "Maybe you should check that."

Léo, already looking in the direction of the living room, stood and crossed to the door in three quick strides. A moment later, they heard him answer the call.

"I hope it's not bad news," Dani said, her dinner suddenly less appealing. She'd learned to fear such calls during Gran's illness.

Ben forced a smile. "It's probably not. You know people can be rude and impatient." But his gaze was on the doorway, and a moment later, Léo appeared, phone to his ear, face ashen.

Malik.

For a second, Dani couldn't breathe. It felt like her chest was being compressed by a vise grip. Blood roared through her ears, and that was what forced her to seize back control of her body—she couldn't hear what Léo was saying.

She sucked in a breath, and as air rushed to her lungs, gasped, "Malik?"

Léo's eyes shot to her, and he shook his head. Ben grabbed her hand and squeezed as she fought back stupid tears of relief.

She forced herself to pay attention, because even if Malik was okay, something was making Léo look like that, and she was likely going to need to be a supportive friend. But Léo was mostly just listening now, occasionally agreeing, until finally he said goodbye and ended the call.

He stared at the phone for a long moment before raising his gaze to look at them. "Uncle died."

Ben immediately stood and went to him, while Dani struggled to process.

"Uncle… you mean Malik's father?" *Fuck.*

Léo nodded, following blindly as Ben ushered him into a chair. "It's… surreal. He had a massive heart attack. Just… keeled over at the dinner table." He shook his head. "I feel… guilty. I don't—didn't ever really… like him. I should have tried harder. Been more respectful."

"You were always respectful of him," Ben said quietly. "That's why we're not there now. It's okay that you didn't like him." He went and got Léo some water, then asked, "Do I need to arrange a flight for us?"

Léo sipped and shook his head. "No, Gabriel said he's already arranged it. I need to call Malik, but…."

Malik.

Dani yanked herself out of her shock. Poor Malik. He and his father had never got on, but still… losing a parent was not something that could just be brushed aside. Should she call him before Léo did? She wanted to, but… Léo was his best friend. The two of them were inseparable. If she had just lost her dad, who would she want to speak to? Ben or Malik?

Both, she decided. And if Malik were there with her, she'd turn right to him. But if a call was necessary… probably Ben first, just because he'd known her dad for so long.

Standing, she went and got her phone and sent Malik a text.

> I'm so sorry. I love you. Call me when you can. <3

Then she went back into the dining room and said to Léo, "I know it's really hard, but you should call him now. He'll need to speak with you." In fact, she was kind of surprised he hadn't called Léo already. He was probably busy with his mother. She looked at Ben. "Why don't you get some things packed?" she suggested. "I'll clear up in the kitchen."

Ben smiled gratefully as Léo picked up his phone and tapped the screen, and Dani began stacking their plates.

When she came out of the kitchen twenty minutes later, Léo and Ben were in the living room, talking quietly. Léo turned to look at her as she entered.

"You should call him," he said immediately. "He was… not himself on the phone. I think it might do him good to hear from you. He said you texted."

Her heart sank, and she chided herself for it. So what if he hadn't replied to her text. His father had just died.

"And then you need to go pack a bag," Ben said.

"The plane will be ready within the hour," Léo added.

Nodding, Dani lifted her phone and went out to the terrace for privacy, tapping the contacts and bringing up Malik's name. Her hand shook slightly as she lifted it to her ear, and again she blinked back tears. Why was she being such an emotional sap? She'd never even met Malik's father, and what she did know about him, she didn't like.

The phone rang, and rang again, then again. She was just beginning to think it might go to voicemail and wondering if she should leave a message or if that would be weird—what could she say, after all?—when the call connected.

And Malik's deep voice sounded in her ear.

"Hello, Dani."

After the initial rush of relief at hearing his voice, she frowned. He sounded… formal.

"Hey," she said, pushing down her reservations. For God's sake, the man had just lost his father. He was probably in shock. "I'm so sorry, Malik. Are you— What do you need?"

"Thank you," he said, again in that oddly distant tone. "There is nothing. Are you well?"

She paused. *Am I well?* "Uh… yeah. I'm… fine. Worried about you, to be honest," she said bluntly.

"Don't worry, I am as well as can be expected."

That tone and his stilted responses were really starting to freak her out. Léo was right, he didn't sound at all himself. She desperately wished she was with him and forced herself to keep her tone light.

"Well, I'll see for myself in a little while. I've just got to grab some things, and then we'll be on our way." Did she even have anything with her that was appropriate for a funeral? What were the customs for Muslim funerals, anyway? She'd need to ask Léo to give her a crash course, or maybe she could google it.

"No."

She was so focused on whether she had anything suitable to wear that she almost missed the soft word.

"No, what?" she asked. He didn't want her to grab some things? It wasn't like she'd miss her flight—five minutes more or less wouldn't make a difference, and she needed her stuff. She wasn't likely to have time to shop for essentials when they arrived.

"No, you shouldn't come."

It took her several long seconds to make sense of that. Her brain, already shocked once that evening, just didn't want to process it.

And then it hurt. A lot.

He's just lost his father, she reminded herself. But shouldn't that mean he wanted her there for support?

This is not about you.

It felt like it was about her. She loved him. If the situation were reversed, she would want him to come. Hell, when she'd lost her gran, he *had* come—and they hadn't been more than friends then.

"I…. Um. You… don't want me to come?"

There was a muffled sound from the doorway, and Dani turned to see Ben there, a shocked expression on his face. Swiftly, he shook his head in apology and retreated inside—no doubt to tell Léo of this latest development.

"My mother doesn't know about you... us. I don't think this is the right time to tell her," Malik explained, still in that stiff voice that was so unlike him.

Relief rushed through her so fast that her knees weakened and she had to sit in one of the chairs at the patio table.

"Of course," she said. "She has enough on her mind right now... but I can come as just a friend, if you like? Nobody has to know we're together." Even as she said it, even as it made perfect sense, that last sentence seemed wrong. *Don't be dumb, Dani.* It wasn't like she was offering to be his dirty little secret—just to be discreet about their relationship while his family grieved. Meeting your son's girlfriend that you didn't know existed for the first time right after the death of your husband would be a *horrible* thing for Malik's mother—and for her, Malik, and the rest of his family.

"That's not fair to you," he said gently, and finally, *finally*, there was a spark of life in his tone, something of the real Malik.

"I can deal with that," she replied bluntly. "What's important right now is you and your family. This is about making things easier for *you*, Malik."

"Then stay there," he said, and his honesty stole her breath. "I will be with my mother, and as merely a casual friend you cannot be here also. You will spend your time sitting in a hotel room, waiting. Please, stay there. I will call you. It will... give me comfort to know you are there, and not mired in the grief and depression here."

"But—"

"Please, Dani. It hasn't been that long since your grandmother passed. I don't want you surrounded by all this again."

She shut her mouth. She could continue to argue, and perhaps she would even wear him down… but to what end? He was right; as just Ben's friend, she wasn't closely connected to the family and couldn't impose on their time of grief. What good would she be doing Malik from a hotel room? If anything, she would just be a distraction to him when he needed to be focused on his family. Léo and Ben would be there, and Charles and Miryam and Gabriel and Celine. They loved him. They would take care of him.

"Okay," she said finally. "Whatever you want, okay? Just take care of yourself."

"I will," he promised. "Text me, please? The way you always do."

That made her feel a little bit better, that he wanted to maintain contact with her. If he wanted "normal" texts, she could give them to him. She would be the bright spots in the midst of difficult days.

"Of course," she assured him. "I love you, Malik."

"And I you. I need to go. We are making the arrangements this evening. Goodbye."

She'd barely finished voicing her own farewell when the call disconnected, and she lowered the phone feeling… a little dazed.

"Dani?"

Turning her head, she met Ben's tentative gaze.

"Hey. Um, I'm not coming with you, so if you want to head off to the airport…."

He came out onto the terrace, closely followed by Léo. "Why are you not coming?" Léo asked, sounding utterly bewildered, which made Dani feel better.

She explained about Malik's mother not knowing about their relationship and the limitations that would put on her presence. "Plus, I think he's a little worried the funeral might upset me," she added. "He said something about Gran, and not wanting me to be surrounded by grieving people." Or at least, she thought that was what he'd meant.

Léo was frowning, but Ben nodded. "Grief hits people in lots of different ways," he said softly. "And we all cope with it differently. For Malik, it may be that what he needs most right now is to know that you're safely here, protected from all the misery—his safe place to come home to, untouched by everything he's going through."

It kind of made sense, but a part of Dani couldn't help wondering if it just meant he didn't need her. That she wasn't important enough to him for him to want her there in times of strife.

This is not about you, Danika, she told herself sternly as she followed Léo and Ben out of the apartment and into the elevator. It was okay—even normal—for her to feel a little discombobulated right now, but it was not okay for her to make Malik's current emotional turmoil a drama in which she played the starring role. He was grieving. He was surrounded by family he wasn't that close to, and he was in a mostly unfamiliar place. It was not up to her to judge the way he chose to cope with that.

There was a chauffeured car waiting in front of the building to take Léo and Ben to Nice. "Get in, Dani," Léo said. "We will drop you off on the way."

She forced herself to laugh. "Don't be silly. It's barely three blocks, and in the opposite direction from where you're going. I'll walk."

Léo looked like he wanted to argue, but Ben took his arm and pushed him toward the car. "You heard her. Let's get moving." The single raised eyebrow he got in response promised they'd be discussing it later, and then Léo bent and kissed her cheek, hugging her hard.

"He will be okay," he murmured to her. "I will call and let you know. Take care."

Sudden tears stung. "Thanks, Léo," she replied gratefully, and then she was enveloped in a bear hug as her bestie wormed his way in. They stood there in a group hug for a long moment, and then Léo said dryly, "Before I met Ben, I would never have been caught dead hugging two people on a public street," and she and Ben laughed as they disengaged.

"It's good for you to be normal sometimes," Ben chided. Moments later, they were in the car and headed up the road. Dani watched them go and tried not to think about how much she wished she was with them, on her way to see Malik. Sighing, she turned and walked in the opposite direction, toward home.

Home. How funny that she already thought of it that way, after such a short time. It truly proved the old adage that home was where the hea—

Okay, that's enough. It's okay to worry. It's okay to be a bit upset. But clichéd bullshit is just not gonna fly.

She stopped and put her face in her hands. This was not her. She was not maudlin or a negative thinker. Moping around was not going to achieve anything.

Dropping her hands, she straightened her shoulders and took a deep breath. She was giving herself until she got home to be a pathetic, emotional mess, and then she was getting on with it.

❧

SEVERAL HOURS LATER, Dani powered down her laptop with a feeling of accomplishment. The first thing she'd done upon getting home was to text Malik. He'd replied immediately with a smiley face and a heart, which had turned her forced cheer into something more natural. Then she'd gotten online and researched Muslim funeral customs, making a list of questions that she'd texted to Léo. The most stand-out fact she'd learned was that unlike what she was used to, in Islam funerals were held pretty much immediately—within twenty-four hours if at all possible, followed by three days of mourning for the family. Léo had confirmed that, telling her the funeral would be the next day.

Next, she'd begun looking into heart disease. Pretty much all she knew was that it was bad and could be genetic, the thought of which freaked her out. Malik's dad had been in his late sixties, which wasn't exactly young, and nobody had said anything about him having heart problems, but still…. It took some research (and several texted questions to Ben) before her fears of losing Malik to a sudden heart attack lessened, but she still resolved to make an appointment for him to get a general checkup when he got back. In the meantime, she'd try to find out if there was a history of heart disease in the family, or if this had just been age-related.

After that, she'd contacted a psychologist friend in Australia, catching her just before she left for work, and asked for any insight she might have on the situation. Dani was very much aware that while Malik had been at odds with his father his whole life, and basically not had him in his life growing up, losing a parent was still traumatic, and she wasn't sure how to approach his grief. She didn't think she should suddenly pretend the man had been father of the year, but neither did it seem right to refer to him disparagingly. Her friend told her to send an email with as much detail as possible and promised to look at it before Dani woke up the next morning.

Finally, she'd methodically gone through and cleared Malik's inbox and social media DMs. He hadn't had anything planned for the rest of the week, not sure what mood he'd be in when he got back from the wedding—was that supposed to have been tomorrow?—and so she didn't have to worry about clearing his calendar just yet. He did have an editing deadline coming up in a few weeks, but she could wait until next week to see if he wanted to talk to his editor about that.

She set her alarm for nice and early so she could text Malik before things got too fraught, and then went to bed.

It was all going to be okay.

CHAPTER TWELVE

alik sat with his head in his hands in the darkened room. It was the first moment he'd had to himself in... he couldn't remember. Hours. Since before dinner. Before....

He took a deep, shuddering breath. How could his father be dead? Surely he was too stubborn to die. Nobody had known there were any problems with his heart. He'd never said anything about pains, dizziness... nothing. How could this have happened?

They'd just been arguing this morning. It had been another yelling match, not the first since Malik had arrived, despite his resolution to be on his best behavior and not let the old man get to him. Malik had finally stormed off, determined not to speak to his father again before his departure tomorrow.

If only he'd known he would never speak to his father again.

If only he'd known a week ago.

A month ago.

Last year.

What would he have done differently? What could he have done to make things better between them? If he had conceded occasionally, maybe they wouldn't have fought so much.

If they hadn't fought this morning, would things be different now?

Malik struggled to push the thought aside. It was unproductive and could only cause him grief, he knew, but a tiny part of him couldn't let it go.

Stress causes heart attacks. What can be more stressful than a screaming fight with the son who disappoints you?

Sighing again, he let his hands drop and sat there, staring into the dimness. He had to get his head together. Léo would be arriving soon, and his cousin knew him too well. He had to be prepared. He didn't want to fight with Léo, but he suspected it would be inevitable. Maybe not right now, but when things began to settle and were supposed to go back to normal and his cousin realized he was firm in his decisions, then there would be a battle.

It didn't matter. He could deal with it. The important thing now was that he finally lived up to his responsibilities to his family—to his *father*. He was only sorry that it had taken his father's death to make him realize it.

Léo and Ben arrived a short time later, and as the car pulled up, Malik went out to meet them. His idiot brother had tried to argue earlier that they should not be coming, that their father had not wanted them there for the wedding and so they shouldn't come for the funeral. His mother had shut that down quickly, sending the idiot off with his tail between his legs. He'd been lucky that all he'd gotten was a verbal rebuke—Malik had seen the looks on Charles's and Gabriel's faces, not to mention Celine's.

As his cousin, best friend, and confidant got out of the car, Malik felt something inside him relax. He and Léo were destined to have some rough times soon, but even so, he would *always* be able to rely on him. That brought him more comfort than a thousand other people could.

He steadfastly refused to think about the one other person who would make him feel better right now, whose presence he longed for. The desire to hear Dani's light voice saying, "Hey," as she ran her fingers through his hair was almost a physical ache.

He would need to get used to that.

In the next moment, he was caught up in a hug so tight, he couldn't breathe. That was okay. He just held on, hiding his face in Léo's shoulder and letting the tears he'd been choking back sting his eyes. Just a few years ago, he and Léo would never have embraced like this. They'd been raised to believe that such displays of affection and emotion were unseemly.

He was so glad that had changed.

Even when they finally let go and stepped back and Malik became aware that his aunt, uncle, Gabriel, his brothers, brother-in-law, and one of his sisters had also come outside and were watching, he was still glad. That one hug from Léo had made a huge difference to his mental state.

He reached out and drew Ben into a hug also, glad to see him even if their friendship was about to come under fire.

"Are you okay?" Léo asked quietly, his dark eyes fixed on Malik's face. Malik let go of Ben and nodded.

"I'm fine," he said. "Although if you'd told me this was going to happen, I never would have believed it would hit me this hard."

"We're here," Ben assured him. "Just tell us what you need. Also, incoming."

It was all the warning he needed. He took a deep breath and turned to see his idiot brother-in-law bearing down on them, an ugly look on his face. Léo swore softly and stepped slightly in front of Ben, but Malik was already moving to intercept.

"Is this what living in Europe has done? You're a faggot now?" his brother-in-law demanded, and Malik felt his face go hard. At least the idiot had spoken in Arabic, so Ben couldn't understand. Léo had, though, and he could feel his cousin's fury at his back.

"Don't be any more of an idiot than you already are," he hissed. The idiot opened his mouth to reply, but a shout from Khalid, their oldest brother—the only one with a brain—cut him off. They both turned as he came toward them, face like thunder.

"You did not just insult your brother, your cousin, and our guest," he said heatedly, and when the idiot made to respond, Khalid made a sharp sound that had his mouth closing again. "Your ignorant views and appalling rudeness aside, are you truly going to cause strife *now*? With Father dead and Mother grieving? Do you want to shatter her already broken heart into tinier pieces? Get inside and stay away from Malik and our guests until you can behave like an adult." He turned his back on him and held out a hand to Léo. "Léonard, it's good to see you."

Léo took his hand, his face an expressionless mask that Malik recognized. Léo had never liked to show anger. "It's good to see you as well, Khalid. I'm only sorry about the circumstances. My deepest sympathies. Uncle will be missed."

Khalid accepted his condolences as the idiot snarled something under his breath and stormed toward the house, and then Khalid turned toward Ben, who hadn't understood a word that had been said but was pale nonetheless, and offered his hand.

"This is my partner, Ben Adams. Ben, Malik's oldest brother, my cousin Khalid," Léo said clearly in French.

"Hello, Ben," Khalid said, also in French, as Ben took his hand and shook it.

"Hello. I'm so sorry for your loss," Ben told him.

"Thank you. Please come inside. Our mother will be glad to see you." The words were ostensibly aimed at Léo, but his glance took in both of them, and Malik wondered briefly if there hadn't been some dissension between his parents about inviting Léo and Ben to the wedding. He'd never known his mother to disagree with his father—not openly, anyway—but there was something about the way Khalid said it....

As they headed toward the door, he shrugged it off. What did it matter now? His father was dead.

LÉO FOUND him less than an hour later. Malik had managed to slip away during the greetings, sneaking off to the rooms that were kept for him despite the fact that he visited rarely, but Léo had obviously only stayed long enough to be respectful before making his excuses, because he barged in now without bothering to knock.

"Please come in," Malik said dryly from where he was seated at an ornate writing desk, trying to put together an email to his lawyer and pretending that his phone was right beside his hand because of coincidence, rather than a desperate wish for Dani to call or text.

You could call her, an insidious voice whispered, but he blocked it out. He couldn't. He needed to start distancing himself now, a little bit at a time. That way it wouldn't be so difficult.

"I've never needed an invitation before," Léo retorted, closing the door and coming to sit in one of the chairs by the window, just feet away from Malik. He turned away from the desk to face his cousin, his throat suddenly dry. He wasn't stupid.

He knew why Léo was there.

Why Ben wasn't.

Léo knew something was going on—something more than just his father having died. And he wanted to give Malik the chance to reach out.

Malik would. But he didn't want to. Léo wasn't going to be happy. *Malik* wasn't happy. But this was the only real option.

"Tell me the truth now, Malik. How are you?"

The question opened a yawning abyss before him. There were so many possible answers.

I'm shocked.

I'm scared.

I hurt.

I'm relieved.

I'm guilty.

I hate myself.

What could he say to make Léo understand the conflicting emotions roiling through him?

"Of course you are grieving," Léo said, seeming to choose his words carefully. "We are all grieving. But, and I say this with all possible respect, the fact of Uncle's death does not change his life."

The words hung between them for a long moment.

"I don't think anyone would blame you for not feeling the depth of grief that perhaps Khalid does," Léo continued softly. "Or if perhaps a part of you felt that this was a reprieve from the constant conflict. But you blame yourself for it."

Did anyone know him as well as Léo?

Malik said nothing. He had no other option. The words were stuck behind the huge lump in his throat. He just stared at his cousin, desperately wishing he could avert his gaze, afraid of what Léo might be reading there.

"I'm sorry that your relationship with your father was not better. I know you've always wanted it to be. I know it always hurt you that it wasn't. And I've always hated him for not seeing how perfect you are. But I've also felt guilty for years, because part of me was glad he was like that, even though it hurt you, because it meant I got you. If we'd been raised in different countries, seeing each other only once or twice a year, my life would have been entirely different, and I'm not certain that would mean better. I—" Léo swallowed convulsively and looked away briefly while Malik's brain struggled to process what he was feeling. "I don't think I would have come out as young as I did without you. I-I feared telling my parents, my friends, even Gabriel—but not you. You were the only person that I knew, right down to my soul, would accept me without hesitation. So while I have always hated Uncle for how he treated you, some tiny part of me was glad, and I must beg your forgiveness for that. If—if I hadn't been so selfish, perhaps our rebellions would have been less... overt, less provoking to Uncle, and he would have realized that he missed you."

Malik sighed. He'd never doubted that Léo was glad to have him in France, not even when they were six years old and barely knew each other, but he hadn't realized his cousin felt so much guilt about it. "There is nothing to forgive. You forget that it was my own nature that got me sent to France. Even if you had been a shy, nervous child who never got in trouble"—they both smirked at the very idea—"it would not have held me back. And yes, it… it hurt that my own father was not able to… to love me as he did my brothers and sisters"—Malik forced the words he'd never spoken through a throat that felt too small—"but I have never regretted being raised in France. If we hadn't grown up together, I would be a different person also." He took a deep breath. This was it. This was the opening he needed. "But you are right that I feel some guilt. My father, for whatever reason, allowed me an incredible opportunity, and all he asked in return was that I return home and put my education to use to support the family. And I defied that, for no reason except that I wanted to. I spent years purposely doing things that I knew would attract tabloid attention, even though I knew how much he would hate that. And we fought constantly because I wanted to maintain a dilettante lifestyle. I regret now that I was so immature. Part of me does feel relief that we will no longer fight all the time, but if I had just stepped up to meet his expectations, I could have had that relief sooner—and without his death."

Léo was frowning. "He wanted to dictate your life," he pointed out. "As an adult, you have the right to decide where to live and how to fill your time, especially when it is neither illegal nor harmful."

Malik spread his hands. "Perhaps. But would it have hurt me to give in occasionally? My brothers and brother-in-law work in the family company, and Khalid is the only one who truly works hard. Perhaps if I had allowed him a nominal victory there, my life would not have been so different." He looked away, unable to meet Léo's incredulous stare.

"Would you have been happy like that? Making a commitment that you didn't fulfill? No," Léo answered his own question. "You wouldn't have been able to do that. Instead you would have worked just as hard as Khalid does—just as hard as *Gabriel* does," he added, reminding Malik that his own situation was very similar, "and hated every moment of it. Try to imagine yourself confined to an office and a schedule, Malik. Working day in and day out solely on your father's business. You would be miserable. How could any loving parent expect—*demand*—that of you?"

Before he could stop himself, Malik said, "Your father demands it of you." Then he closed his eyes, because arguing with Léo was not what he wanted—and he knew it wasn't really true.

Silence. Malik opened his eyes to see his cousin studying him thoughtfully.

"I'm sorry," he blurted. "Uncle Charles still nags you about taking a role in the company, but we all know he'd keel over in shock if you actually agreed—and then tell you not to be ridiculous." For all Charles Artois's bluster about Léo's life, he was inordinately proud and perhaps secretly envious of his younger son.

"Malik," Léo said softly, ignoring him, "what have you done?"

Malik sucked in a deep breath. "I need to meet my responsibilities," he declared.

"You said that before. What responsibilities are you referring to? Because I have never known you to shirk any."

"It's too late for my father to see me fulfill his wishes for me, but in respect for him, I need to do it anyway."

Léo's jaw dropped. Malik forged on.

"I'm taking my place in the company."

"*Are you insane?* No, wait"—Léo held up a hand—"I apologize. That was uncalled for. But Malik, have you thought this through?"

Malik nodded. "I have. I have been wasting my education and contacts, Léo. All my father ever wanted from me was for me to proudly represent the family, and I defied him. The least I can do now is put my immaturity behind me."

It was Léo's turn to close his eyes. When he opened them, they bored into Malik like lasers. "Are you listening to yourself? Really *think* about what you're saying."

"I'm not like you," Malik protested. "You're using your natural talents and your education. You're a brilliant financial manager, and you've ensured that none of us will ever want for anything, ever. I do *nothing*, Léo. I had an education that millions dream of handed to me, and I'm wasting it."

"Shut *up*," Léo roared, leaping to his feet. "Stop saying that! You are not wasting your education *or* your life. You're a successful author, for the love of God!"

The words struck like an arrow, but Malik ignored the pang of pain and shook his head. "You know my father would never have accepted that." He saw in Léo's face the exact moment he understood.

"You're giving it up? I thought you meant to work in the company and write as well, and I wondered at your sanity, but… you love writing. How can you just…?"

Malik met his cousin's gaze squarely. "I need to fulfill my responsibilities."

Léo nodded. "Okay. This is a very stressful time. I think we should leave this discussion for now, and perhaps come back to it when we have paid Uncle his due respect. Don't… don't do anything irrevocable for now. Perhaps wait until you have discussed it with Dani."

Malik flinched.

Léo dropped back into the chair as though his knees had failed.

The silence drew out as Malik tried to find the words to explain.

Finally Léo said, "Let's not talk about this anymore. You have a lot on your mind. I'm sure that once the funeral is over and you've had time to process, you'll be thinking more clearly."

Malik ignored the implication that he was out of his mind.

"But you need to call Dani," Léo warned. "She's worried about you. Whatever you decide later, you need to reassure her now."

He nodded. Léo was right.

He'd call her tomorrow.

❧

MALIK STARED AT HIS PHONE. He'd been staring at it for what felt like forever but could only have been a few minutes.

It had been four days since his father had died, since Léo and Ben had arrived, since his cousin had told him he was insane. His father had been laid to rest, the mourning rites had been completed, and Léo and Ben were barely speaking to him.

It was all his own fault. He was handling everything poorly.

He'd spoken to Dani each day, but acting was not his forte, and she'd known there was something he was keeping from her. Despite that, she'd been nothing but supportive— she'd sent him the texts he loved so much and had answered his calls on the first ring, no matter what time he called. If he needed to stay longer with his mother, she'd said, she could get in touch with his agent and editor and get him an exten-sion on his deadline. Or she could do that anyway, and that way if he decided to visit more often, he would have some flexibility in his schedule.

That had been yesterday, and he'd known then that he couldn't continue. Couldn't let her keep thinking that he was worthy of her love, of her caring.

"I'm not coming back," he'd blurted, without anything to soften the blow. "I mean… I'm staying to take up a position in the family company. It was what my father always wanted."

Dani hesitated, clearly taken aback. "Okay," she'd said slowly. "I imagine that's going to slow your writing down a lot. I can tell Elise, but she'll probably want to talk to you herself."

Malik closed his eyes. His stomach hurt. "No, I mean yes… I'll need to talk to Elise. But I won't be writing anymore. This is a full-time commitment, and I can't dishonor my father by splitting my attention."

"You're giving up writing?" Her voice rose in pitch, the tone incredulous. "Are you— I mean. Um. Okay. You need a break. You need to…. What would you be doing at the family company? I have trouble seeing you in a desk job, Malik."

"Yet that's what my future holds." He tried to say it lightly but failed utterly.

"Why?" This time she didn't try to be diplomatic or understanding. "Why are you doing this? I get that you're grieving, that you miss your dad and wish the two of you had seen eye to eye more. But you're not a corporate whatever, Malik. That's going to make you miserable."

"I think you're wrong," he lied, because the conversation was already too hard. He was exhausted and his chest was burning with the knowledge of what he was about to do, and he couldn't stand to argue with her about his career path, too.

He heard her take a deep breath, and then she said, "I guess you know yourself better than anyone," and he knew she was back to being considerate of his feelings because she thought he was vulnerable right now. He wanted to curse and shout at her to not be so nice. "I'll tell Elise that you need an extension because of your father's death, and that for the same reason you're not sure when you'll be submitting the next book. If you decide not to return to writing, that's fine, but if one day down the track you find that you can balance your new career with being an author, then at least you won't have burned any bridges." She forced a chuckle. "And I guess I'd better start looking for a new job. If you're not actively writing, you probably won't need me full-time. Where…. Um. Are you going to be based in Monaco still? Or maybe Paris?"

It was the opening he needed, but he didn't want it. She was planning her job hunt—the hunt his decision was forcing on her—based on where he would be. She was planning to relocate—*again*—to be with him.

He hated himself.

"I will be here," he heard himself say, but couldn't add anything else. He was the worst kind of man.

"Oh." Expectant pause. "So… um, I guess that might be a problem, since I don't have… I mean, I can't—"

"It might be best if you went back to Australia."

The silence this time was razor sharp. Malik forced himself to swallow, bit back the desire to take it back, to tell her he would be home in a few days, hell, a few *hours*. To just run away and go back to the life he really wanted.

"Let me be entirely certain I understand," Dani said, her voice cold and calm, none of the previous uncertainty in evidence. "You're moving to Saudi Arabia to begin a new career, and in your wisdom have decided that there's no place for me in your new life, so you're dumping me?"

"I—"

"Shut up, Malik. I'm still talking. What reason have you chosen for our breakup? Is it my personality? My background? My ethnicity or religion? I never would have thought those would matter to you, but then I never would have thought you'd tell me you loved me and that we had forever together, and then less than two weeks later change your mind."

"It's not—"

"If your next word is going to be 'you,' then I strongly recommend you never finish that sentence," she snapped. "You're a disgrace, Malik. I get that you're grieving. I know you and your dad never had a great relationship and part of you probably feels responsible for that. If you really want to make a grief-clouded decision to uproot your life and change it completely, that's something you have to work through. But what you're doing to me now… either you never really loved me in the first place, which makes you an utter pig for pretending you did, or you're letting this stupid, misplaced sense of guilt you feel right now mean more to you than me and my feelings, and *that's not okay*. I'll leave the key with the concierge."

She'd hung up and not answered when he tried to call back. She'd ignored his texted apologies and attempts to explain. And when he'd seen Ben an hour later, he'd been treated to a glare so freezing cold that he'd actually shivered.

Which brought him to now. It was the first day since he and Dani had started dating that he hadn't received a text from her. And it was painful.

He had to get used to it.

Every day would be like this from now on.

A sudden, overpowering hatred of his phone took over him, and he threw it across the room. It sailed through the doorway, narrowly missing Khalid, who ducked and turned to watch as it crashed into something.

"I think the screen may be cracked," he reported, but didn't go to pick it up. Instead he entered the room and closed the door. Malik eyed him warily. He and Khalid got along fine, but they'd never been close. Khalid was five years older, a solemn, serious man whose priorities in life were his family and the company. Their father had been bursting with pride for his oldest son, and while Khalid had always been kind to Malik when they were children and, unlike their father, had accepted his adult life, Malik knew his brother didn't really understand him. Khalid was happy with a quiet life of work and family. Malik was not.

Or he hadn't been. He was sure he'd get used to it. After all, he was in his thirties now. Wild oats had been sown, or whatever the expression was. People settled down as they got older, and it was his turn.

"I needed a new phone anyway," he quipped, trying to sound lighthearted and *not* to think about the last time he'd broken his phone by throwing it across the room—after a conversation with his father. "Is everything well?"

Khalid spread his hands and sat—incidentally, in the same chair Léo had occupied only a few days before. To Malik, it felt like it had been years. "Things are as well as they can be," he said fatalistically. "It will take time for everyone to settle into the new normal."

His brother looked tired, Malik realized as he sat at the desk. He was now the head of the family and responsible for the company—and their mother. She was a strong woman, but she was accustomed to leaning on her husband, and the adjustment would be difficult for her. "Please don't hesitate to ask if there's anything I can do to make it easier," he said, hating that he had to offer. If he'd made more of an effort with his family over the years, they'd be comfortable leaning on him now. They would ask for assistance without him having to offer first.

Leaning back in the chair, Khalid studied him. "Thank you," he replied quietly. "I am grateful. There are some things I will send your way."

"Of course." It wasn't much, but it was a beginning. "I'm glad you're here. I need to speak with you."

"About taking a role in the company?" Khalid raised an eyebrow, a faint smile crossing his face as Malik started.

"Who—? Léo told you." He sighed.

"Actually, no," Khalid denied. "Léo has said nothing. Nobody said anything. You are not as good at hiding your feelings as you think, Malik. And you have been asking questions… I guessed that you might be considering some changes."

A tiny spark of something warm ignited in his chest. His girlfriend—ex-girlfriend—hated him, and his best friend wasn't speaking to him, but it seemed his brother knew him better than he had always thought. Perhaps there was a chance for them to be close.

"You guessed correctly. I plan to move back here and take a position in the company, the way Father always wanted me to."

Khalid nodded. "We would of course love to have you so close. Mother has missed you greatly, and I have always wanted time to become better acquainted with you. And if you want to join the company, I will happily arrange it. But, Malik… I don't need you to."

It was a slap. Of all the reactions he could have predicted, being told he wasn't needed had never been on the list. As Malik scrambled for something to say, Khalid held up a hand.

"You will be most welcome, and I have no doubt at all that you would be a strong asset. But the company is not in trouble. Things are going well and will continue to do so. If this is a step you are taking because you are concerned, then don't be. If it is something you genuinely want, then I welcome you with open arms. You would be a much better executive than Mahmud and Fareed. But I don't want you to sacrifice your own desires—if this is not where your heart lies, you would end up miserable, and I don't want to be responsible for making my baby brother unhappy."

Malik sagged back in his chair, unable to stay upright.

"I…." He met his brother's steady gaze. "It was what Father always wanted."

Khalid sighed and stood and began pacing. "Father…." He stopped, paced some more, then turned to face Malik. "I loved Father. He and I were very much alike in many ways. But one thing I never understood was why he could not be more accepting of you. Malik, there is nothing wrong with you or your life. Father couldn't understand you, and he had no tolerance for things he couldn't understand. You wouldn't fit into the box he had designed for his children, and so he tried to force you there. Mother made the right decision sending you to France. As much as we all missed your exuberance, if you'd stayed, Father would eventually have crushed out the best parts of you." He sank into the chair again. "A friend of mine from university is a psychologist. I have spoken to him at length about you. The first time was years ago, when you and Léo were being kicked out of the best schools in Europe. I could not imagine breaking the rules to such an extent as to be expelled from school, and I was worried. I told my friend all about you, but he wasn't concerned. He says you are a free spirit, a creative soul. You think outside the box and to a large extent, don't like to be constrained by rules and regulations. I am the opposite; I take comfort from guidelines and boundaries. So did Father. If it didn't fit what he knew and was comfortable with, he had no use for it. That was why he tried so much to dictate your life. Why he wanted you to come back and take a role in the company. Why he put this ridiculous idea into Mother's head that you needed to marry."

Malik winced. He'd been steadfastly ignoring the fact that when he moved back, his mother would take it as free rein to matchmake.

Khalid sat forward. "It has always been a great regret to me that I don't know you well. But I know that even while being expelled from school after school, you managed top marks. I know that you and Léo graduated from Oxford with honors. I know that you are highly intelligent and competitive, and I am *certain* that you do more with your time than just attend parties, especially within the past five or so years." He smiled wryly. "I just haven't been able to find out what—and believe me, I've tried."

This is it. Malik swallowed hard. He'd wanted acceptance from his family; here was Khalid, offering it to him on a silver platter. He just had to take it.

But he doesn't know yet what you do.

What if he thinks it's business related and this disappoints him?

What if he thinks it's stupid? Not good enough?

Father never would have accepted writing as a career.

Why do I even need to say anything? That's over now.

But then another part of him spoke, stronger than the rest.

Khalid has faith in you. He doesn't think you're just a layabout, even though all the evidence points toward it. He knows you're capable of more, that you've done more. He'll be proud of your achievements because you achieved them.

He took a deep breath. He'd always felt like an outsider in his own family. Had always wished he could be closer to them. Here was his brother, offering him that opportunity. A chance to confide in him. What it came down to was how much he trusted this—trusted Khalid.

"I'm an author," he blurted. "I write books." And then, because Khalid looked surprised and he didn't know how to take that, he began a rambling monologue about his books and his pseudonym and his career, until he wanted to strangle himself so he would just *stop talking.*

By the time he managed to stumble into silence, Khalid was grinning.

"You are a published author! See, my friend was right—

you're a creative soul. I don't read much, but I will buy your books and read them all—and Mother will, too." He stopped. "How did we not know this already? You must have taken great pains to keep it secret."

Malik's lips twisted in a wry smile. "I did," he admitted. "I wanted my career to be separate from the rest. My public life has not always been exemplary, and I didn't want my books tainted by that." The memory of some of the wilder parties he'd been to floated in his mind. "And… Father would never have approved."

"True." Khalid nodded. "So you're a writer. This is your vocation. Wouldn't it be much harder to write if you are also working for the company?"

"I—I would stop," Malik admitted. "Father would never have approved." Suddenly, he felt like an idiot. Was he trying to gain his father's approval? That was never going to happen. And even if it could, did he truly want to give up the things that made him happy just to please one man? A man who should have loved him regardless of his life choices? Khalid, his brother, had admitted to not understanding Malik or his life, but was still enthusiastic about it. Had still expressed a wish for them to be closer. Why couldn't his father have done the same?

His volatile relationship with his father was not because of him and his choices. It was because of his father's inability to accept anything different.

He looked up and met Khalid's gaze. His brother was watching him intently, a small smile on his face.

"I'm an idiot," Malik said, and Khalid laughed.

"Perhaps. Does this mean you're not coming to work in the company after all?" he teased.

Malik shook his head. "And I don't think I'll move here either, although I will come and visit more," he promised. In fact, he'd come for a nice, long stay and get to know his siblings better as soon as he had his next deadline out of the way. He could take a month or two off before he began work on the next book. Dani had already said—

He groaned. *Fuck.*

"What's wrong?" Khalid asked, alarmed.

"I'm an idiot," Malik repeated. "An absolute imbecile." He pressed the heels of his palms against his eyes. "Shit." He lowered his hands and saw Khalid watching him with an expression of sympathy.

"A woman?"

Malik snorted. "How did you guess? I... shit, she's never going to forgive me."

Khalid settled back in his chair. "Tell me about this woman."

CHAPTER THIRTEEN

Once the fog of grief and stupidity had cleared from Malik's brain, he decided he wasn't doing anyone much good in Saudi Arabia right then and begged Uncle Charles for a lift home with them. His uncle had studied him with a sharp gaze, then asked, "Are you back to yourself?"

Malik winced. Had he been so obvious? To everyone? "Yes. I was confused, but I'm not anymore."

Charles nodded. "And you will fix things with Léo? And Ben?"

"I will," he promised. *And Dani.* "It might take a while, though."

A shrug. "It takes as long as it takes. You and Léo should not be at odds." He'd paused then, and an expression of discomfort had crossed his face. "Malik, I think of you as my own. If there is anything…."

It was a shot to the heart for Malik. Uncle Charles had never been an affectionate or demonstrative man, not with him, not with his own sons. But Malik had never in all the years he'd lived in Charles's home felt excluded. Charles had praised him and scolded him just as he had his own children.

"I know, Uncle. Thank you."

Charles cleared his throat, and the moment had passed.

Next had come a long chat with his mother. She had at first been devastated that he was leaving so soon, but when he'd explained why and promised to come back as soon as he could, her distress had morphed to acceptance—and scolding. His mother, it seemed, was thrilled that he had a career he loved, was bursting with pride at his accomplishments, and was dying to meet Dani. She'd lectured him for half an hour about his foolish decision to end the relationship and then made him swear that he'd call her as soon as he'd fixed it so she could "meet" Dani.

He'd agreed, part of him all warm and gooey with the knowledge that his mother cared so much, although another part wished he had her confidence in his ability to fix his relationship woes.

Then he'd gone in search of Léo.

Unfortunately, it seemed Léo was not ready to talk to him.

Dani listened with half her brain as Ben ranted in her ear. He was legit pissed at Malik, and she couldn't blame him, since her own anger had resulted in her needing to buy Léo and Ben some new glassware. Thank God she'd restrained herself to the everyday stuff in the kitchen. It had still been expensive to replace, but not as much as the crystal would have been.

How could he have done this to her? What was he thinking? Didn't he know that she would have gladly moved to Saudi Arabia if that was what he truly wanted? He didn't, though; she knew him well enough to know that. Malik was not cut out for a desk job and a rigidly defined life. But if he'd wanted to try, she would have supported him every step. That he hadn't wanted her there—*didn't* want her there, didn't want *her*… that hurt.

Fuck hurt. It eviscerated her.

She took a slow, deep breath, careful not to let Ben hear it hitch. She was *not* going to start crying again. It felt like she'd done nothing but cry or scream or throw things since she'd hung up on Malik last night. She was exhausted, wrung out, and the skin under her eyes was almost raw. She was stuffy-nosed and basically a mess, which was why she'd said no when Ben suggested FaceTime or Skype. He was already worried about her, had been since the moment she called and told him she needed somewhere to stay. He didn't need to see the physical traces of her misery—not yet, anyway.

"…back in the early afternoon," he said, and she tuned in. "Léo said not to even think about dinner; he's already arranged for a meal to be delivered, and we're just going to veg all night."

Right. Ben and Léo were coming home tomorrow. They'd originally planned to stay until the end of the week, but things were apparently very tense with Malik, and Charles had some business commitments he couldn't get out of. Miryam was staying, though, to be with her sister.

"It'll be good to see you," Dani told him, even though it hadn't even been a week since they'd left. It felt like longer, like an eternity since she'd seen Malik.

Pushing the thought aside, she asked, "Do you want me to meet you at the airport?" She would have to take one of Léo's cars, but she could manage it.

"Nah, we'll get a driver. I was thinking, we should go back to the UK later this month. This is the best time of year, weather-wise, and you wanted to see more of Scotland, right?"

"Yeah," Dani said, her throat tight. Scotland. Australia. The moon.

Anywhere but Monaco, where all her memories of Malik were.

❧

THE ATMOSPHERE on the plane was grim. Malik hadn't managed to speak with (and profusely apologize to) Léo and Ben the night before, and when he'd approached them earlier, Léo had shaken his head and put in earbuds, while Ben had glared so vehemently that Malik had decided a tactical retreat was in order.

But he had to act, and soon. In just a few hours the flight would be over, and it would be much harder to apologize and explain then. He knew Léo would eventually forgive him, and he wished he could give him the time he clearly wanted, but the longer he left things with Dani, the worse it would be. He'd checked with his building concierge, and she had taken a bag and gone, leaving the key and the rest of her belongings. He was absolutely certain that she would have gone to Léo and Ben's apartment, and there was no way in hell he'd be able to speak to her unless he got them on side.

Now was the time. They were a captive audience; with the plane in the air, the only place they could go that had a lock on the door was the lavatory, and he was fully prepared to shout through the door if necessary.

Taking a deep breath, he rose and crossed the cabin. His uncle gave an approving nod as he passed, and Gabriel merely seemed concerned, but Celine had a sour look on her face. She liked Dani and adored Ben and Léo and was taking this whole affair as a personal affront.

He'd win her back over. She'd always loved him, too, had called him her unofficial brother-in-law.

How was I ever such an idiot as to think I didn't have a real family?

He sank down into a chair opposite the sofa where Léo and Ben sat. Ben glanced up from his phone and glared, but Léo remained focused on the book he was reading.

"I'm sorry." There, that was a good beginning. Ben's expression turned suspicious. He wasn't prepared to relent just yet. Léo didn't look up. "I let my insecurities get the best of me. I made stupid decisions and acted rashly. I was wrong. I was especially wrong to let my decisions affect the people I love most."

Léo put his book down and met Malik's gaze, but said nothing.

"As you can see"—Malik spread his hands—"I came to my senses and will not be leaving my home and throwing away the career I love. Oh," he remembered, and turned to face the rest of the cabin. Charles, Gabriel, and Celine were watching avidly, not even pretending not to eavesdrop. "I'm an author. I write suspense thrillers under the name Raphael Martin."

Gabriel's jaw dropped. Charles blinked. Celine gasped. Malik left them to their shock and turned back to Léo and Ben.

"I'm sorry. I'm sorry I didn't listen when you tried to help me, to show me I was being... misguided. I'm sorry I didn't trust your judgment and wait before making big decisions. But most of all, I'm sorry that I dragged you into the middle of my personal issues."

Ben sighed. "You were doing so well until that last one," he chided. "Malik, you're family. We don't care that you drag us into your personal issues. What we care about is that you did something really *stupid* for no good reason."

"What are you going to do now?" Léo asked.

"Beg," Malik replied promptly. "My first priority is to

repair the damage I have done. If you both can't forgive me yet, I will wait, but when we get back to Monaco, I will start groveling to Dani."

"Oh?" A dangerous gleam lit Ben's gaze. "So you don't think she'd be best off going back to Australia?"

Malik winced. "Hell, no. The absolute dumbest thing I've ever done was tell her that. Even if I had lost half my mind and decided to work for the company, I should have asked her to come with me, not broken up with her." He shook his head. "It's not even been two full days, but already…." No texts, no calls, not even the knowledge that she loved him and was waiting to sustain him. His chest felt hollow. Instead, he had to live with the fact that he'd hurt her—deliberately—and at the same time hurt himself.

"And you're prepared to grovel?" Ben seemed oddly intent. Malik met his gaze.

"I will crawl for as long as it takes her to forgive me."

"What if she never can?" Léo asked, and Malik jerked.

His chest tightened, and suddenly he couldn't breathe very well. Forcing himself to suck in air, he said, "Then I'll need to learn to live with my mistakes. But I still need her to know how sorry I am that I hurt her, and that she is the best part of my life."

A heavy silence descended on the cabin. Malik kept breathing, one breath at a time. That was what he needed to focus on, one moment, one breath, until it was time for the next one.

Finally, Léo broke the silence. "You're an idiot," he said, and there was a note of fondness in his voice that sounded more wonderful to Malik than anything else ever had.

DANI WAS SITTING out on the terrace, staring into space, when she heard the front door open. They were back. A minute later, Ben came out and sat beside her.

"Hey."

She turned to see him studying her with a frown on his face.

"You look like shit," he said bluntly.

She shrugged. "It's been a rough couple of days. It'll get better." Maybe. God, she hoped it did. She didn't think she could handle this pain forever. None of her previous breakups had felt like this, not even when she was in Year Ten and her boyfriend dumped her because she wasn't ready to have sex with him. She'd always thought that the betrayal she'd felt then would be the worst she'd ever feel, because she'd lost part of her innocence that day… but even it paled compared to this.

How could Malik so easily have left her behind?

"Yeah… so…." Ben hesitated. "We need to talk."

What now? She raised an eyebrow. "Are you breaking up with me too?" If she joked about it, that would make it better, right?

Judging by the flat look Ben shot her, he wasn't in the mood for humor. She sighed. "Okay, what is it?"

Ben swallowed hard. "Malik came to his senses and decided not to move to Saudi and take a corporate job," he said fast.

For a moment, her heart soared. *Yes!* Then she remembered that he'd made the choice in the first place, that he'd *hurt* her, and the oppressive grief returned.

She said nothing.

Ben winced, then pressed on. "He wants to talk to you."

"I don't want to talk to him," she said, but oh, this was going to be a problem. He was Léo's cousin. They were closer than brothers. They saw each other almost every day; Malik was used to coming and going from this apartment like it was his own. How could she live here without causing upset to everyone's lives?

"Then you don't have to," Ben promised. She waited for the rest, but he said nothing else, and eventually she sighed.

"Go on, tell me."

"No." His voice was firm. "I'm on your side, Dani. Always."

She leaned over and hugged him tight. She'd really missed him over the last forty hours since Malik had broken her heart, even if they had spent a lot of that time talking. "I know," she muttered into his shoulder, feeling him squeeze. "But tell me anyway." She pulled back. "I know you, Benji. If you thought it would hurt me more, you wouldn't even be thinking about it."

"Damn straight," he declared, then took her hands. "You don't have to talk to him," he reiterated, "and I don't actually think you should talk to him today. But I do genuinely believe he's sorry. That he made a stupid, grief-fueled mistake. He's ready to grovel, do whatever it takes. So... if you want to think about it. I mean, you can just say no and it's all done. Or you can say no for now, and see how you feel in a few days or a few weeks."

Dani thought about it. "Is he here?"

Ben hesitated, then nodded. "But I don't think he actually expects to see you today," he added. "I mean, he wants to, but we all kinda thought you'd just tell him to fuck off." He grinned, and she smiled back.

"Part of me wants to," she admitted. "But that's mostly because I hurt, and I want him to hurt too."

"He does," Ben said quietly. "Even before he came to his senses, he was... not himself. Since then.... I know Malik pretty well, and I can see that he's suffering." He shrugged.

"He brought it on himself, literally, but that doesn't mean it doesn't hurt him."

"Yeah." She stared out over the ocean. "I'm not ready to see him today," she said finally. "But it's not fuck off. Not yet, anyway."

hree days later, Dani was ready. She'd done a hell of a lot of soul searching, and although she wasn't sure if she was quite at the point of forgive and forget and happy reunion, she was at least prepared to hear what Malik had to say.

She thought.

Taking a deep breath, she left her room and went down the hall to where Malik was waiting in the living room. Ben had knocked on her door, told her Malik had arrived for his daily "is Dani ready to talk" visit, and upon hearing that she would come out, had promptly corralled Léo and declared they were going shopping.

He hadn't even made a face as he said it.

So she knew the apartment was empty aside from her and Malik. Just them. Alone. With no option but to talk. About them.

It almost made her want to turn tail and hide in her room.

Instead, she made herself walk calmly—on the outside, at least—into the living room. Malik turned from where he was standing by the doors to the terrace, and for a long moment, they just stared at each other. He looked tired, maybe a little thinner. There were very fine stress lines around his eyes, which she may not have seen if he hadn't been standing in the bright sunlight. It had been only two weeks since she'd last seen him, but they'd clearly taken a toll on him.

"Hey," she said finally, when she couldn't stand it anymore.

"Hello. Thank you for seeing me," he replied, and he sounded so formal that she wanted to cry. This was not how they were together, even before they were together. Everything was different now.

She hated that.

"No problem." She had to keep things moving along. If she had time to think, time to look at him and remember how much she missed him, she might cry.

No more fucking crying.

"Do you want to sit, or...?" She gestured to the couch, and then took a seat in an armchair. He hovered for a moment, then folded abruptly to a seated position.

And they sat in awkward silence.

Should she say something? What the hell should she say? What *could* she say?

"I'm sorry," he blurted, his voice so unexpected that she jerked. "I-I don't know what I can say that will…. I'm afraid to try and explain, because I don't want to make this worse. If it can even *be* worse. I'm sorry." He shook his head. "That's what I need to say first. I'm sorry. I was wrong. I should have listened. I should have waited until I was thinking clearly to make any sort of decision. I should have done anything except hurt you. I'm sorry."

Dani felt tears well up and she hated herself. Damn her for being so emotional. Taking a deep breath, she spent a moment regaining her composure.

"Thank you," she said finally. "I appreciate that saying

sorry isn't the easiest thing to do, but it really means a lot that you've said it."

His beautiful dark eyes searched her face. "Good," he said quietly. "I never, ever wanted to hurt you, and I will always regret that I have. I… I hope that you can forgive me. That we can… can possibly start again?"

Her heart began beating faster.

"Start again?" What did that mean, exactly?

He shrugged awkwardly, a movement that looked wrong on him. "We could start dating again. I… I want things back the way they were. I want to plan our future and start plotting how I'm going to ask you to marry me, but I understand I need to earn that back. So, we could start again. Last time we jumped in with both feet, but if you wanted to take it slower this time…. I'll do anything you want."

Dani forced herself not to react, to take a deep breath and think carefully about what he was saying. It wasn't dumb. They had jumped into things very fast. They'd taken things from friendship to being all coupled up and living together literally overnight. Maybe it would be a good idea to start again and go more slowly.

What did she want? That was the important thing, right? What she wanted? That was what her gran had always said: work out what you want and then get it.

So what did she want?

She wanted a fulfilling job.

She wanted friends and family in her life.

She wanted Ben around.

She wanted a home that made her happy to live in it.

She wanted Malik.

Meeting his gaze, she said, "I think that's a good idea. Let's start again."

For a moment, he sat frozen, then he grinned. "Okay. Okay, good. That's… thank you. I promise, you won't regret this. I love you." His eyes widened, and Dani felt like she'd been punched in the stomach. "I'm... I didn't mean to pressure...."

"It's fine," she managed. "I mean... I get it." She sucked in a deep breath and mentally pulled on her big girl undies. "I love you too. But... I need space to think. So we're going to go slow."

He nodded. "Whatever you want."

She nodded.

They sat awkwardly.

"Uh... how are you?" she asked abruptly, because he'd just lost his father and had a brain fart.

He smiled faintly. "I'm okay. It's... odd. I spent so much of my life wishing my father would just... I don't know. Leave me alone? Go away, somehow. I never wished him dead, though, and now that he is, I have so many regrets. I-I always wanted him to see me—see the value in me. And knowing he'll never be able to do that made me a bit.... Well, I lost perspective. The truth is, even if I had fallen in with his plans, we likely would still have argued all the time. We were just very different people, and he was too stubborn to accept anything that wasn't exactly what he wanted." He sighed. "I have to accept that I'll never have the relationship I wanted with my father." He seemed to brighten then. "But I talked with my oldest brother, and I think we'll be closer now. I told him and Mother about my books, and they were both enthusiastic."

Dani grinned. "That's great! I'm so glad. You're so talented—your family should know how amazing you are."

"Thank you. I likely wouldn't have done it if you hadn't made me see how different things could be if some people knew."

"And it worked out for the best. Are you going to stay in contact with your brother now?" She hoped so. She and her sibs weren't particularly close, not like she was with Ben, but it was still great having them in her life. She wanted that for Malik.

"Yes. I'm going to go for a long visit once I've sorted this deadline and we're… I mean, when things are…."

"When we've sorted things out between us," she suggested, and he nodded gratefully.

"Yes. I'll go and stay for a while, make my mother happy, get to know my siblings and their kids better."

They spoke for a little while longer about stupid, inconsequential things, until finally Malik stood to go. Dani hated herself for the rush of relief, but seriously, could things have been any more awkward?

Yes.

They could.

She knew that because as they both hovered by the front door, they became more awkward.

What was the etiquette for saying goodbye to your boyfriend who broke your heart but who you were giving a second chance?

In the end, she rose on tiptoe and kissed his cheek. "I'm glad you're back," she said honestly, and he smiled at her, a little sadly—perhaps remembering the last time they'd said goodbye, before he'd gone to Saudi Arabia, and how very different it had been.

"I am too."

⚜

LATER THAT NIGHT, he texted her.

This is how I feel right now.

Below was a link to YouTube. She tapped it curiously and

was taken to a video of a singing telegram group serenading a laughing woman. The lyrics heavily featured words like idiot, stupid, mistake, forgive, and love. She grinned the whole way through, and then at the end, the person filming called, "Tell us what he did!"

The laughing woman looked straight at the camera and said, "He donated my Prada handbag that I saved for a year to buy to charity."

The video ended, and Dani winced. Sure, she would have been pissed—*very* pissed—if that had been her, but it wasn't exactly the same as being unceremoniously dumped with no warning.

But there were mitigating circumstances. He'd been grieving. Fucked-up by his childhood insecurities. And he'd come to his senses and apologized. Profusely. She'd agreed to give him another chance—didn't that mean she actually had to try? Because if she didn't actually want this to succeed, she needed to just tell him now and end the farce. There was no point in them starting over if she'd already decided she couldn't let it go.

She stared at the screen of her phone. Wherever Malik was, the message would be showing that she'd read it. So what did she want to say?

> If you donated my Prada handbag, it would take more than a singing telegram to save you.

Not that she had a Prada handbag. She'd seen the prices on those things, and even when she'd been in the mood to splurge hadn't been able to justify it to herself, no matter how pretty they were.

Three dancing dots appeared on her phone.

> What about a singing puppy?

The next link was to another home video, this one of a woman off-screen, presumably the one filming, singing an Ed Sheeran song, and the adorable golden retriever on the screen barking along to the tune. When the woman stopped singing, so did the dog, and when she started up again, the dog did too, doing an all-over shimmy that looked remarkably like dancing.

This time, she laughed out loud.

> Okay, the singing dog would save you.

A light knock on the doorframe got her attention, and she looked over to see Ben smiling tentatively.

"I heard you laugh."

"C'mere." She shifted over on the bed and waited for him to join her before playing the dog video again. Ben was making kissy noises at the screen within the first few seconds.

"Where did you find that?" he said when the video ended, now holding her phone. She took it back.

"Malik sent it."

Silence. She looked over at her bestie, a little surprised by his reaction.

"Malik's sending you dog videos?" The shock on his expression was mirrored in his voice. She shrugged.

"He's sucking up. Look." She showed him the text string, which meant rewatching the singing telegram video too.

Halfway through, another text from Malik popped up, and before Dani could dismiss the notification, Ben had snatched her phone away.

"Dinner tomorrow night?" he read aloud and then jumped off the bed and danced out of her reach, tapping at the screen.

"Ben! Give that back! Don't you dare reply!" She lunged

after him, but for a man who often tripped over his own feet, he proved to be incredibly good at texting while dodging her. She chased him around the room and out into the hall, where they both crashed into Léo, who'd obviously come to see what all the commotion was about.

They managed to remain standing, but Ben dropped her phone, which she swooped up before he could detangle himself from Léo.

"Doesn't matter," he gloated. "I sent it."

"You're sending messages from Dani's phone?" Léo asked incredulously. "Are you a teenager?"

Dani swiped the screen unlocked, then opened the messaging app. Sure enough, he'd sent Malik a text.

> Only if you bring me a puppy.

"Really, Ben?" she said acidly. "Of all the things you could have written, that's what you decided on? He wants a dog," she told Léo, then turned and went back into her room, leaving her bestie to plead his case.

Her phone dinged in her hand.

> Really?

She could only imagine the look on Malik's face as he'd typed that.

> No. Sorry, Ben got my phone. He's gone now. Dinner tomorrow sounds great.

It really did. More so when he texted back with laughing emojis.

> I would buy you a dog if you wanted one. I like dogs.

Aww. She liked dogs too. What made her stomach go all jittery, though, was the implication that he needed to like dogs because he'd be seeing a lot of hers.

Not that she had a dog.

> Maybe one day. Let's have dinner first.

THEIR FIRST STARTING-OVER date was at the same place they'd had their first date. Dani was hit hard by memories of how happy she'd been the last time they'd been there, and it made her feel better. More confident.

Malik, on the other hand, seemed nervous.

"What's wrong?" she finally asked after he straightened his cutlery for the fifth time.

He pulled a face. "I'm wondering if I made a mistake deciding to come here," he admitted. "We had so much fun last time, but…."

"You're afraid that's going to remind me that you did a stupid thing," Dani finished for him, and he nodded. "Relax. It does, but it also reminds me of how amazing you can be and how good we are together."

He visibly relaxed, then studied her, a small smile tugging at his lips.

"What?" she asked, suddenly self-conscious.

"I really want to kiss you."

The words floated between them, and Dani swallowed, her throat suddenly dry. She met Malik's gaze and saw there all the love and desire he'd always shown her.

So she leaned forward.

Eyes widening, Malik seized the opening and leaned in also. The kiss was awkward, with the table between them, and over far too soon, but for Dani, it was perfect. She licked her lips, enjoying the lingering taste of him. His eyes darkened.

"We should do that again later," she murmured, feeling bold, and then Malik grinned wickedly. Butterflies exploded in her stomach.

The rest of their meal went perfectly. Somehow, the kiss had dispelled all the awkwardness between them, and they fell into their old rhythm. It was so good to have that back—the comfortable baseline but also the push-pull of sexual attraction.

It wasn't until they left the restaurant and got into the car—the slight chill to the air prevented Dani from suggesting they walk—that she made her decision.

Maybe she and Malik had zipped through the early stages of their romance—but that was only because they already *knew* each other. They'd been friends, close friends, for months, and acquaintances for years. Nobody could say they'd rushed their relationship; it had just switched tracks from friendship to romance. If she truly meant to put her hurt behind her, what was the point of keeping him at arm's length? He was sorry. He'd made that abundantly clear. He'd also made it clear through his actions that he intended to make it up to her. That he loved her. That he respected her.

She wanted to be with him. Part of her was scared of being hurt again, sure, and only time would heal that, but... did she have to spend that time apart from him? Wouldn't she regain her confidence in their relationship much faster if they were together?

What it came down to was, she was ready to move on with Malik.

"Let's go to your place."

Malik looked at her searchingly. "Are you sure?"

She nodded. "This idea of starting over was a good one. I

needed it. It gave me a chance to really think through what's happened and what I'm feeling. But I love you. You made a really stupid mistake, and you're sorry. I'm probably still going to feel insecure for a while, but only time will fix that, and it's dumb for us to be apart when all I really want is you."

He closed his eyes briefly and sighed. "Thank you. I am sorry, I swear, and I'll do anything you need—everything—to make you confident in us again. If you'd needed to just date for the next year, I was ready to do that. But I'm so glad we don't have to. I've missed you so much."

Grinning, Dani pulled him in for a kiss.

The drive home was short but seemed to last forever. Dani waved at the night shift concierge as they passed, the same one she'd given her key to not that long ago as she'd dragged out her overnight bag with tearstained cheeks. He looked surprised to see her, then grinned broadly.

They kissed in the elevator all the way up to Malik's floor, then stumbled into his apartment and left a trail of clothing from the door to the bedroom.

By the time they made it to the bed, they were both incredibly aroused, breathless, hands roaming, mouths seeking, but despite that, their lovemaking was unhurried. If Dani had thought about it ahead of time, she would have assumed that this first time together again after weeks apart would have been rushed, desperate, but instead, it was about rediscovery.

The rough silk of his skin under her hands.

His mouth on her, tormenting her.

The heat and scent of him, so familiar, so dear.

As she kissed her way down his body, her hand stroked slowly over his cock, delighting in the soft-over-steel feel of it and Malik's reactions to her touch. She'd missed this so much.

"Hello there," she murmured, and licked the head of his dick.

Malik hissed. "Don't, Dani… I'm too close. I want to be inside you when I come."

She blinked, surprised, and then a grin spread over her face. "Already?" He'd never lacked stamina before.

"I've missed you," he admitted, hauling her up to kiss her mouth.

"Yeah," she agreed, and their kisses slowly went from gentle and loving to urgent and needy. When Dani realized she was dry-humping his thigh, she tore away and scrambled in the nightstand for a condom. It took her only moments to roll it on him, but the act was so familiar that her body's reaction was Pavlovian, her arousal skyrocketing.

His eyes darkened as he felt her wetness on his leg, and he sat up in a smooth motion, his lips finding hers and his hand going to her pussy. Just a light touch of his fingers was enough to have her back arching.

"Hurry up," she panted, all thoughts of slow and romantic out the window. A good breeze would make her come right now.

Grabbing her hips, he maneuvered her to straddle him properly and lowered her onto him. Dani closed her eyes as he slid inside and wrapped her arms and legs around him. Finally.

Malik rocked back and forth, and although the movement was slight, she was so turned on that it may as well have been full-on thrusting. It took only a few moments before the first tiny tremors began, and then every muscle in her body tightened as she flew over the edge. The sound Malik made as she came around him was indescribable, and then his whole body clenched in her arms.

When finally they were spent, Malik blew out a long

breath and toppled backward against the pillows, bringing her, still held securely in his arms.

Lying on Malik's chest, still breathing hard, Dani closed her eyes and smiled. This was where she was supposed to be.

EPILOGUE

Malik looked around at his friends and wondered what he'd done in a past life to deserve this kind of happiness.

Dani was at the center of it all, of course. Over the past year, her presence in his life had made everything better. He'd worried for a while that living and working together would become a problem, especially since Ben was the only friend she really had in Monaco, but then one day she'd announced that she'd joined a local women's business association. Technically it was only for business owners, but when she'd explained her situation and that she was responsible for the entire "business" function of Malik's career, they'd made a special exception. Since then, she'd really connected with several of the women, and they met—whether officially or unofficially—at least once a week. She'd also gotten involved in fundraising efforts through Celine, who hadn't had as much time as usual to devote to her favorite charities once she'd had her second baby. The organizational duties required fit Dani perfectly. It meant some occasional travel, but since Malik could work anywhere and generally attended many of those fundraising events anyway, their lives still meshed together naturally.

Meanwhile, her efforts with his social media and advertising had been repaid beyond their expectations. Sales had shown a steady increase, and his last book had surprised them all by debuting much higher on the best-seller lists than any of his others. His publisher had been so pleased that they'd committed a lot more marketing budget to his next release… which was due to happen any minute now.

It had been Dani's idea to have a release party to celebrate. He'd protested that a book release was nothing new for him, but she'd insisted.

"Last time it was just us," she'd said, the twinkle in her eye reminding him how they'd celebrated. "And before that, it went pretty much unmarked. But you have people who love you and also love any excuse to open a bottle of champagne, so let's take advantage of that and have a party."

He'd given in, not quite as reluctantly as he'd made it seem, and the look she'd shot him was a good indication that she knew that. The guest list had been limited by the fact that very few people actually knew he was an author. Léo and Ben were there, of course, and Lucien and Si. His aunt and uncle and Gabriel and Celine had flown down from Paris for the night, toddler and baby in tow, and he'd spoken earlier in the evening to his mother, Khalid, and all of his sisters, who'd expressed regret that they couldn't be there but promised to come en masse for a visit soon. He was actually looking forward to it—he'd been back to Saudi Arabia several times in the past year, getting to know his family better and letting Dani get to know them too, and he rather liked the controlled chaos that occurred when everyone was in the same place. Surprisingly, he'd even managed to convince serious Khalid to take part in subtly tormenting Mahmud and Fareed. It had been a bonding experience.

"Come on, stop being all introspective!" Dani grabbed his hand and dragged him into the center of the room. "Let's crack open the champers."

Laughing, he went to do as he was told, and soon they'd passed around glasses.

"A toast!" Dani declared. "Someone make a toast."

"Why don't you do it?" Ben asked, but she shook her head.

"No, I'm rubbish at them."

"I'll do it." Léo stepped forward, and they all settled down and waited for him to speak.

"I have never doubted Malik's brilliance—I took advantage of it many times to get in and out of trouble in our youth." A cackle of laughter interrupted him, led by Malik as he fondly remembered those times. "When he told me he was writing a book, I never doubted that he would succeed, even when he was unsure. We kept it a secret for a long time, and it always pained me that I couldn't shout his brilliance from the rooftops. Now, with book number eight, I finally get to raise a glass and say, to Malik, my cousin the author. I am so very proud of you."

"To Malik!" Glasses clinked and his friends and family drank, but Malik couldn't move. He choked down emotion and met his cousin's gaze. Léo smiled as he made his way over.

"That was a beautiful toast, Léo," Dani said, rising on tiptoe to kiss his cheek. "Thank you."

"It was entirely my pleasure. Thank you for arranging tonight, Dani. I've wanted to celebrate my clever cousin for a long time."

Still, Malik couldn't speak.

"He deserves it." Dani slid an arm around his waist and leaned into him. The familiar warm weight of her was all he needed to regain his composure. He wrapped his arm around her shoulders and kissed her head.

"Who would have thought," he said to Léo, "that we both would have found such happiness from you picking up a tourist in the casino?"

Dani elbowed him in the side, but Léo laughed.

"I heard that," Ben said, joining them, "and I think it deserves a toast of its own. Everyone," he raised his voice, "to getting drunk on champagne and meeting the love of your life!"

There was a great deal of laughter and confusion as everyone toasted—even Aunt Miryam, who disapproved of drunkenness and didn't drink alcohol—and then someone turned on music and food was brought out.

Malik smiled and looked down at Dani at his side.

"I love you."

She grinned at him. "I know."

Thanks so much for reading *Between The Covers,* and I hope you loved it!
If you haven't already read the other Met His Match books, you totally should! Meet Dani and Malik for the first time in *Charming Him,* where cheapskate Aussie tourist Ben is swept off his feet by sophisticated French billionaire Léo.

To talk spoilers and hear what's next, join the chat in my Facebook group, RoMMance with Becca & Louisa
Or you can subscribe to my newsletter to get all updates and access to bonus scenes: https://bit.ly/LouisaMBonus.

Interested in exclusive bonus scenes, serials, early chapters, and artwork? Check out my Patreon: https://www.patreon.com/louisamasters

Spirited Situation
Vortex Conundrum
Conduit Crisis
Gateway Catastrophe

Here Be Dragons
Dragon Ever After
The Professor's Dragon
The Dragon Experiment
Conspiracy of Dragons

Hidden Species
Demons Do It Better
One Bite With A Vampire
Hijinks With A Hellhound
Sorcerers Always Satisfy
Hidden Species Box Set

Met His Match
<u>Charming Him</u>
<u>Offside Rules</u>
<u>A Christmas Chance (novella)</u>
<u>Between the Covers (M/F)</u>

Joy Universe
I've Got This
<u>Follow My Lead</u>
<u>In Your Hands</u>
<u>Take Us There</u>

Novellas

Fake It 'Til You Make It (permafree)

One Golden Night

O Hell, All Ye Shoppers

Out of the Office

After the Blaze

Blokes Down Under Novella Collection

ABOUT THE AUTHOR

Louisa Masters started reading romance much earlier than her mother thought she should. As an adult, she feeds her addiction in every spare second. She spent years trying to build a "sensible" career, working in bookstores, recruitment, resource management, administration, and as a travel agent before finally conceding defeat and devoting herself to the world of romance novels.

Louisa has a long list of places first discovered in books that she wants to visit, and every so often she overcomes her loathing of jet lag and takes a trip that charges her imagination. She lives in Melbourne, Australia, where she whines about the weather for most of the year while secretly admitting she'll probably never move.

http://www.louisamasters.com